VYKOR

Star-Crossed Alien Mail Order Brides

SUSAN HAYES

ABOUT THE BOOK

Looking for love on all the wrong planets? Try the Star-Crossed Dating Agency.

Born without a dragon's spirit, Vykor has no magic, no clan, and no reason to stay on his homeplanet of Romak. He's come to Earth to research old legends – and maybe even find acceptance.

This book contains an executive assistant in need of assistance, and a researcher who is about to discover that love doesn't come with instructions.

SERIES READING ORDER

Star-Crossed Alien Mail Order Brides

Joran

Vader

Kash

Tarjen

Torel

Radek

Karos

Jet

Vykor

Vykor (Book #9 of the Star-crossed Alien Mail Order Brides Series)

First Print book Publication: October 2019

Cover Design: crocodesigns.com

Editor: Dayna Hart

Published by: Black Scroll Publications

ISBN: 978-1-988446-56-1

As always, this story is dedicated to my Mum and Dad, for their love and support of their sometimes-crazy daughter, and to Karen, for so many years of laughter and friendship.

CHAPTER ONE

OF ALL THE times to forget my motion sickness pills.

Lily pressed her face to the cool surface of the plane's window, watching the ground roll by beneath them. Her boss' private jet might have every comfort imaginable, but it was still vulnerable to turbulence, and so was she.

They were below the cloud cover now, and she could see the city through the rain-splattered glass. Everywhere she looked, she saw grey. Grey streets, grey clouds, even the daylight had a pall to it, like it had been filtered through smoky glass.

As dull as it looked outside, she'd trade a week's worth of lattes for a breath of fresh air right now. If it would get them on the ground faster, she'd consider offering up her firstborn. Not that there was any chance of her conceiving a kid any time soon. First, she'd need to be dating someone, and she didn't have much luck when it came to romance. Her co-worker, Megan, theorized it was because she only dated nice, safe guys, and kept trying to set her up with guys from her gym or dojo.

Megan was a freaking bodyguard who Lily was privately convinced was some kind of terminator. She was tough, smart, and immune to bullets. Lily had seen her get shot once, and instead of falling over like a normal person, Megan had just sworn louder and kept firing at their attackers. Megan had saved their lives that day, while all Lily had done was get on the radio and scream for help. She just wasn't cut out for a life of danger. Especially not in her love life. She'd had enough danger in her personal relationships to last a lifetime.

The plane pitched again, and she gripped her armrests tighter. "Definitely not in my love life, and especially not while traveling!"

"I'm missing all the best parts of that conversation. Care to back up and start at the beginning?" Megan drawled from her seat, her lips parted in an ear-to-ear grin.

"Nope. Inside voice malfunction. Please disregard." Lily flapped a hand in the air.

Everyone laughed and started their pre-landing rituals. They all had them, and after so many years together, Lily knew exactly what they were. Hanna would store her laptop and then do a quick check of her hair and makeup so that she came off the plane looking polished. Megan wouldn't bother at all about her appearance. Instead, she'd walk the length of the plane to limber up after sitting still for hours.

Lily spent the last few minutes going over their itinerary and reviewing her notes. Hanna was an easy woman to work for, and Lily took pride in ensuring that her employer's days proceeded as smoothly as possible. That included providing Hanna with any information she might need, including statistics and the names of anyone she might meet in the course of her meetings. Over the years, they'd worked out a system that allowed Hanna to focus on the bigger picture while Lily handled the small details. Today, every detail might be important.

Hanna Dewan ran a charity organization that specialized in rescuing women and children from hostile areas and relocating them. Until now, all those relocations had been to other countries on Earth. If this meeting went well, then some of those women would be travelling to a distant planet to find their new start.

When she'd been hired, she'd never imagined all the places she'd visit or the people she'd meet. She'd also never dreamed that she'd become close friends with the woman who signed her paycheque. Hanna and Megan were like the sisters she'd never had - a family she'd chosen for herself.

Lily exhaled in relief when they finally touched down. It didn't matter where they were landing—London, Vancouver, or a landing strip deep in a war zone—Megan treated every arrival the same way. She went first and assessed the area. Once she was satisfied, she'd wave Hanna and Lily forward.

Lily retrieved their suitcases while waiting for the all clear and then took her place behind Hanna, positioning herself in a current of fresh air from the door.

Hanna gave her a sympathetic smile. "Ready to be off this plane?"

"Very."

"All clear," Megan called from outside. "But soggy. Welcome to the west coast, ladies. Land of liquid sunshine."

"She is way too happy to be home," Hanna murmured over her shoulder as she left the plane.

"You'd think after so many Toronto winters, she'd be used to the snow." Lily didn't bother to lower her voice. She wanted her friend to hear her.

"Never going to happen. Snow sucks." Megan started down the metal stairs.

Lily made her way down the stairs carefully, juggling all three suitcases with the ease of long practice. Megan needed her hands free, and Hanna was already meeting with the alien ambassador they'd flown here to meet.

She got a good look at him once she was down the stairs. She'd seen his photo and interviews as part of the research for this meeting, but he was even more handsome in person. Dark hair, movie-star looks, and a suit that looked like it cost more than her last paycheque. He was holding an umbrella out for Hanna while they greeted each other and then made introductions.

Another man was with them, but she was too busy dealing with the luggage to pay much attention. It wasn't until she heard Jet say the other man was from Romak that she looked up, surprised. She hadn't expected there to be a Romaki dragon here today.

A tall, blond man with the perfect amount of Hollywood scruff and amazing eyes turned from Hanna and walked toward her, smiling. "Hello. Do you need some help with those?"

She tried to speak, but it came out as an awkward squeak of surprise. "Oh! Uh, I mean yes, that would be helpful. Thank you."

He held out his hand. "I'm Vykor. You must be Ms. Dewan's assistant, Ms. Ashton."

She stared at him for a handful of mortifying seconds before her brain started working again and she took his hand. "Hello, Vykor. Please, call me Lily."

She was pleased at how rational and normal she sounded despite a sudden urge to ignore his outstretched hand and kiss him instead. *What's wrong with me?*

The second their hands touched, her brain short-circuited again, and when he raised her hand to his mouth to kiss the back of her knuckles, a shiver ran down her spine that had nothing to do with the winter weather.

"Lily." Vykor tipped his head to one side and

smiled, his dazzling eyes gleaming silver and gold. "That's a flower, isn't it?"

"It is. My mother's favourite flower. Which is why she named me for it. What does your name mean? If it has a meaning, that is." She babbled, trying to ignore the lingering feeling of his lips against her hand. Normally, she didn't like being touched, especially not by guys, but apparently the ghost of trauma's past was making an exception for Vykor.

He paused. "It has a few meanings. It can mean something that is lost or someone who is searching for something."

"And you're a researcher, right? Here to document the legends about dragons from our cultures to see if they could be lost members of your species. So, you really are looking for something."

He took her suitcase from her and moved the umbrella he held to shelter her from the rain. "You know who I am?"

She caught the note of surprise in his voice. "It's my job to know anything my employer might need to know."

He considered that for a moment, then nodded. "You're her researcher." His voice wrapped around her like a caress, and she forgot all about the chill wind and rain.

"That's part of it. My job is pretty boring, though. Not like yours."

He gave her an amused smile. "Most beings think that about mine, too."

"But you study *dragons*!" She regretted her words the second they left her mouth. Of course it wasn't a big deal to him, he *was* a freaking dragon.

"I feel the same way about learning the history of your species." Much more interesting than my own. I've been reading about Atlantis. I have a theory…" He trailed off and inclined his head toward the others, who were already moving to a waiting limousine. "Shall we join them?"

"I'm so sorry. Of course."

Vykor started walking, keeping the umbrella over her as they went. "Why would you be sorry?"

"Because I was talking too much, and you're getting soaked standing around listening to me."

"I'm not concerned by a little dampness." He lowered his voice to an amused murmur. "We Romaki aren't as delicate as the Pyrosians."

She glanced up at him, barely suppressing a giggle. "That's not a very diplomatic thing to say."

"Ah, but I'm not officially a diplomat. I'm here as…" he paused as if searching for the right word. "Jet's wingman?" Is that right?"

This time, she couldn't stop herself from laughing. "I understand your meaning, but you might not want to say it quite that way."

Vykor frowned. "Why not? I thought it was a military term."

"It has a slang meaning, too. If you're acting as someone's wingman, then your job is to help them score with a woman. Usually, in a social setting like a bar."

Vykor's dazzling eyes filled with amusement, and he glanced over at Jet. "Until he meets his mate, Jet has no need of a wingman. And unless things go catastrophically wrong, he shouldn't need my help after he's met her, either."

She looked at Jet, then back at Vykor. "I don't suppose either of you need any help in that department."

Vykor blinked and almost tripped over himself. "You don't?"

"Well, no. I mean look at you. Guys like you shouldn't have any trouble attracting a woman's attention on any planet."

She expected him to laugh, or at least smile, but he didn't. Instead, his eyes darkened and his jaw tensed. "The females of my planet do not share your opinion."

His voice was as tight as his jaw. She stopped briefly, released the handle of one case, and touched his arm, her shyness losing out to her need to fix what she'd done. "Then the females of your planet are idiots."

He smiled and ducked his head, and for a second she could have sworn she saw him blush. "Thank you."

"For telling you the truth? You don't need to thank me for that." She started blushing, too, and they walked the last few steps in silence, neither of them looking at the other. One day, she'd figure out a way to talk to a good-looking guy without making a fool of herself. Today was not that day.

WHAT IN THE *name of Solun's frostbitten balls is wrong with me?* Vykor took one last breath of winter air before getting into the vehicle. It didn't do anything to cool the sudden flash of heat that had kindled inside him the moment he'd spied the little blonde female. He'd been so taken with her he'd almost walked away from their other guests before introductions were made.

The female was small and curvy, and the spiralled curls of her blonde hair blew around her face in a chaotic tangle he wanted to bury his fingers in. It didn't make any sense. He'd been attracted to females before. He might be a dragonless male, but he was still male. Even so, he'd never felt anything like this.

He entered the limo and belted himself in, forcing himself to keep his focus on that simple task instead of watching Lily as she claimed the seat across from him. She wore a simple skirt of deep blue that came down to mid-calf and boots that rose past the hem of her skirt, completely hiding her legs. Her jacket covered the rest of her, frustrating his desire to see more.

He did his best to ignore her effect on him, but every few minutes he stole a glance across the limo, and each time he grew a little more concerned. Her windburned cheeks had faded to a sickly pallor, and her lips were pressed together in a hard line. He wanted to talk to her, ask her what was wrong, but he couldn't do that without pointing out her discomfort, which would only embarrass her.

When they got to the embassy, he'd talk to her again and make sure she was alright. Did she need to see someone at the medical center? Maybe she just needed something to eat. Whatever it was, he'd make sure she got it.

It took him a few seconds to recognize how insane he sounded, even to himself. She was almost a stranger, and Jet hadn't brought him along so he could look after Ms. Dewan's staff. He was supposed to be helping to ensure this meeting went smoothly.

Jet wanted him to take on a more active role at the embassy, to try his hand at diplomacy and working with the humans. Vykor wasn't sure he had the knack for it, but Jet believed he did, and he was happy to try any job that would allow him to stay on Earth. Here, he'd found some level of acceptance. Back home, there was no such thing. How could there be for a Romaki born without a dragon's spirit?

He fisted a hand at his thigh as an unexpected rush of anger rolled through him. He had to take a few deep breaths and repeat the litany he'd been taught as a child three times before the anger faded.

He couldn't remember the last time his control had slipped like that.

He relaxed into his seat, taking note of what was going on around him. Hanna was seated beside him, talking in soft but animated tones to Jet about what the process would be for the women she hoped to eventually bring to Pyros. Jet was explaining that the women would have full citizenship before they even set foot on the planet, and it was clear Hanna was thrilled by the news. Her passion and enthusiasm showed in every word and gesture. He'd read her biography, knew that she was dedicated to her mission, but reading about someone wasn't the same as sitting beside them as they spoke.

He listened to their conversation but didn't join in. Things were going well and despite Jet's concerns, Vykor didn't see any signs that Hanna needed reassurance. No doubt there would be a moment he could step in and give an honest opinion as someone with no ulterior motive. It wasn't *his* planet suffering a catastrophic lack of females. Besides, Romak was only just recovering from a planet-wide civil war. None of Hanna's refugee females would want to go there. It would be too much like the places they were fleeing.

He looked over at Lily again and caught her watching him. She blushed and dropped her gaze immediately, denying him a longer look at her lovely violet eyes. He leaned forward to say something to her when Megan shouted a warning to hold on.

There was a second of silence, and then everything happened at once. There was a jarring impact, the screams of living beings and twisted metal, and the vehicle careened wildly and threw everyone against their restraints.

It was over almost as quickly as it started. Across from him, Lily looked shaken but unhurt, and he uttered a sigh of relief. Megan was issuing orders, arranging for help to be contacted before declaring she was going to go outside to take a look.

That's when she looked at him for the first time. "If

anything happens, can you transform and get the others out of here?"

Shame choked him, but he opened his mouth to reply. She needed to know he couldn't help. Not like that.

He never got a chance to answer. The driver's partition lowered, and everyone started speaking at once.

Their driver, Kyle, dropped a canister through the gap. The partition rose again, sealing them inside. The doors all locked, a synchronized clunking noise that boomed in the suddenly silent space.

A white vapour poured out of the canister and Vykor knew exactly what was happening – they were being gassed. The problem was, he didn't know what the hell to do about it. Though he was stronger than most humans, he wasn't strong enough to tear off a door or shatter one of the windows, which were made of projectile-resistant glass.

Megan was sprawled across Lily, hammering at one window with powerful two-footed kicks, but it wasn't going to be enough. Dizzy and disoriented, he undid his seatbelt.

Something heavy sagged against his side, and he groggily realized that Hanna was slumped against him. He should have been able to move her easily, but his arms were too heavy to lift, and he slumped in his seat.

Who turned up the gravity?

CHAPTER TWO

LILY WOKE from one nightmare into another. She'd been dreaming, drifting through dark recollections of a childhood full of angry words and hard fists, only to wake to find herself bruised and bound, her stomach roiling and her head pounding like a ten-kilo centipede was tapdancing on her head.

It took her several seconds to work past the blind fear that tried to consume her, but she managed to push it aside. She needed to stay focused on what was happening around her. Megan had taught them both how to deal with a crisis, what to do if the unthinkable happened and they wound up captured or on one of their trips to the more dangerous parts of the world.

She took stock of her situation. Something blocked her vision, a hood, she guessed, but her senses still worked. It didn't take long for her to figure out she was in the back of a vehicle, a large one, based on the way it rocked and swayed. Her arms and legs were bound with thin hard strips. She was on her side, her hip and shoulder aching where they pressed against the floor. Whoever had put her in here hadn't been gentle.

The ride was bumpy enough to jounce and jar them every few minutes, and after one of the nastier bumps, someone uttered a low groan. She thought it was Hanna, and she rejoiced at the knowledge she wasn't alone. A second later, her joy was squelched by guilt. She shouldn't be happy her friend had been captured, too.

"Hanna?" a male voice called out, then there was a thump and a grunt of pain.

Another male, this one's voice full of anger and hate, spoke, "No talking, ya alien asshole."

Well, that answered the question of who was behind the attack. There was only one group who hated aliens enough to do something like this: The Humanity First movement. They were a group of vile, vicious men who somehow thought that the women of Earth belonged to them and only them. They blamed the Pyrosians for their lousy luck with women, as if any woman would date a violent, brutal man with no manners when they might be matched to a Pyrosian male who wanted nothing more than to find their true mate and treat them with adoration and love for the rest of their lives. It was a no brainer, which was why she'd signed up for the dating service as soon as she'd learned about it. It sounded like paradise, which was why Hanna wanted to send more women there, where they'd finally be safe.

She kept listening, hoping to hear from some of the others.

"What about the other one?" another male asked.

"The dragon? Boss didn't say anything about him. We were only supposed to be bringing back three of them."

Her heart sped up a little. They'd taken Vykor, too? Then, the rest of what the man said sank in. Hanna, Jet, and Vykor were here, which meant Megan wasn't with them. That wasn't good. Where was she? What had they done with her?

The men were still talking, and she tried to push aside her fear to pay attention to what they were saying. Something about Vykor being a freak with no magic and no ability to shift. Well, that explained why he hadn't transformed already. He couldn't.

She felt badly for the Romaki. It had to hurt to hear himself described that way.

The men with them were rough, and evidently prone to violence. During the ride, both Jet and Hanna were struck for speaking, but despite the risk she eventually found a moment to speak up and let the others know she was okay. It was all she could do. These were dangerous men, and it wouldn't be smart to piss them off.

By the time the truck stopped, she was too queasy to do anything but remain still and quiet as rough hands lifted her to the ground and cut away the bindings on her legs. It took all her focus to stay on her feet, a task made harder by the hood that covered her face and the occasional shove from one of the men escorting her. She could hear gulls cry somewhere nearby, and the air was heavy with the smells of the sea. Not that it helped much—Vancouver was a coastal city. Nothing she sensed gave her any real idea where they'd been taken.

The unsteady tickity-click of high heels hitting concrete ahead of her had to be Hanna. A door swung on rusty hinges, and the footsteps faded away. Lily squared her shoulders and kept walking. Even if they separated them, she wouldn't really be alone. She could do this.

"Watch your step," a male voice rumbled.

She lifted her feet with care for a few steps, allowing her to avoid tripping over the threshold of a doorway. Voices in the distance, someone barking orders. "You and you, escort the prisoners to their cell. I'm going to go get something to secure the creature."

The creature. She wished she knew where Vykor was so she could do something. Touch his arm. Say his name. Anything to offer a bit of comfort, no matter how small. For that matter, she could use a little comfort herself. She was sick, scared, and achy from the rough treatment and uncomfortable ride.

"This way." Someone gripped her shoulder and hauled her in a new direction. Someone nearby tripped and landed hard. She heard the telltale thuds of boots striking flesh, triggering memories she didn't want or need right now. "Stop it. Please stop."

"You an alien lover?" Someone snarled, the voice full of malice.

"What I am is cold, sick, and scared. Please, just take us to our cells so I can sit down. I really don't want to throw up inside this hood."

The same gruff voice that had told her to watch her step spoke up. "Bossman didn't say nothing about beating up the alien. Just told us to take it to the cell and secure it. You want to get him pissed at you?"

The other man answered with a surly growl, and she was led forward again.

"Step up," the man told her.

She did so, and the flooring changed again. Metal maybe? She couldn't be sure.

Someone grabbed her again, spun her around, and lifted the hood from her face. The light was dim enough it didn't hurt her eyes, but it still took a few seconds for her to get her bearings. Before she could take in any details, a blade flashed in front of her eyes and she stepped back in fear.

"Relax. I'm just going to cut you loose." The man across from her was older, with dark hair and a weatherworn face. His grey eyes were flat and cold, and his expression was unreadable.

She stayed frozen until he'd finished cutting through the straps that bound her arms, her eyes never leaving the knife.

Once she was free, he pointed to a shelf-like bunk welded to the back wall of her cell, and she went over to it and sat down.

"Good. I like a woman who knows her place. You

stay quiet and well-behaved and you'll be on your way home soon enough."

She hated herself, but she forced herself to nod her head slightly. She'd be well behaved…until it was time to fight. Megan had taught her that, too.

Two men brought Vykor in, while another heaved a battered office chair into the cell. It was one of the high-backed styles executives seemed to favour, well-worn but still solid looking.

"Sit." One of the men shoved Vykor into the seat, while another held it steady, so it didn't go rolling backward on its wheels.

In a few minutes they had him tied to the chair, though the arms were too thick for them to use more of those awful straps and they had to use rope instead. That was good. Rope she could deal with.

They didn't even take his hood off before leaving.

"Don't talk to it. Don't feed it. And if it bothers you, you let us know. We'll take care of you," the one who had cut her free told her as he left. She didn't like the way he said it, or the way his eyes lingered on her once he was outside. It took two men to haul a heavy gate made of welded bars along a track and into place. The gate was locked into place, and then they were gone, leaving her alone with Vykor.

She rushed over to him. "Are you alright?"

"You're not supposed to be talking to me."

"Then we better keep our voices low, so they don't hear us. And you didn't answer my question. Are you okay?"

He uttered a wry chuckle. "Depends on your definition of the word. How about you?"

"Not even close to okay, but at least I'm not tied to a chair." She pulled off the black hood that covered his head, and for a moment she just stared. Somehow, he'd gotten better looking since the last time she'd seen him. Either that, or being terrified was playing hell with her perceptions.

He lifted his head and smiled at her. "Hello again."

Her heart skipped a beat. "Hi."

———

She is so lovely.

Not the first thing he should have been thinking, considering their situation, but apparently being close to Lily turned off all the logical parts of his brain.

"Do you think the others are okay? I'm worried about them. Megan, too. They didn't bring her with us."

He looked around the metal box they were trapped inside. There was a rough bunk welded to the back wall, a squat, beige object in the corner, and not much else. "I heard the males say that Jet and Hanna weren't to be hurt. They'll be alright."

"I guess I should be more worried about us." Her hand touched his shoulder. "I wish they'd stop being so mean to you."

"I'm used to it." He rolled his shoulders in a dismissive shrug.

Her smile faded. "No one should have to get used to

being treated like that. Is it true, what they said?" She blanched. "Not the way they said it. You're not a freak, or a creature, you're Romaki. But…one without magic?"

She'd heard. He swallowed his shame and gave a small nod.

"And your people gave you crap about it? I thought the Romaki were an advanced species. All enlightened and wise." Her mouth formed a moue of disgust. "Doesn't sound very advanced to me. That's the same petty nonsense we have here on Earth."

"It's not the same thing. I represent something that shouldn't be. Daga and Solun, the Gods we follow, represent the two clans, Fire and Snow. Every Romaki is claimed by one of the Gods at birth. Gold eyes, fire dragon. Silver eyes, snow dragon."

"And you have one of each colour."

"Exactly. I don't belong to either God, which means I have no clan. My parents abandoned me outside a shrine to both Solun and Daga when I was still an infant. No one wanted anything to do with me."

Instead of looking at him with horror or pity, Lily cocked her head to one side and pursed her soft lips thoughtfully. "Who decided you didn't belong to either God?"

"The priests."

"The ones who raised you?" Her voice was tinged with shock. "They told you that? You were a child!"

"They're priests. They won't lie. Not even to protect a child." The priests who raised him hadn't all been comfortable around him, but most of them had been decent, if distant.

"How do you know they were right? What if they're wrong and you belong to both Gods. I mean, if you weren't claimed by either god, wouldn't your eyes be some other colour?"

He stared at her in shock, too shaken to speak for what felt like forever. Eventually, he managed to dredge up some words from the shattered mess she'd made of his head. "That's not—. I mean, it couldn't be. Romaki only have two eye colours."

"And they're supposed to be of the same colour, right? So, that rule is already out the window."

"That's not how it works." He wasn't even sure why they were talking about this. He knew what he was, and this conversation wasn't doing anything to address their current problems.

She straightened her head and flashed him a smug little smile. "Says the guy who just said no one on his planet knows how he wound up with eyes two different colours."

"Two eye colours and no dragon. No magic." He tried to gesture with his hands and grimaced in frustration when he remembered he was still tied to the chair. "If I had even a small amount of magic, we wouldn't be here right now. I could have stopped this from happening." *I could have protected you.* The thought came with another irrational flash of anger.

"What could you have done?" she asked.

"More than I did." He'd never forget the moment

Megan had asked him to protect them, assuming he could wield magic like every other Romaki.

"Even if you could turn into a dragon, you couldn't have done it inside the vehicle. You'd have squashed us flat if you'd tried. Do your people have a spell for magically removing gas from the air?"

"I...uh. Well, no. But I'd have thought of something. Summoned my dragon's strength to tear off the door, maybe."

She didn't look convinced. "We had less than a minute from impact to losing consciousness. None of us managed to do much, not even Megan, and she's a trained professional. I think you should cut yourself some slack. All I managed to do was try to call 911, and I didn't even manage that before I passed out."

"Are you always this logical?" After everything she'd endured today, her calm assessment and lack of anger astounded him. Most beings he knew would be reacting emotionally - lashing out, seeking to cast blame or at least vent their frustration. The only being he knew with that kind of emotional control was him. And today, even he was having trouble with his temper.

Her demeanour changed instantly. Her shoulders tightening, gaze dropping to the floor. She exhaled once, then lifted her head again, her expression shuttered, now. "Sorry."

He didn't know what just happened, but he didn't like the change one flaming bit. Again, he tried to move his hands, only to be frustrated by his restrains. He needed to touch her, Comfort her. Bring back her smile.

"What are you sorry for, *razdi*? I meant it as a compliment. Since you don't seem pleased by my question, I should be the one apologizing."

"Oh." Her expression softened slightly. "Most people don't like it when I'm too practical."

"One thing you can be sure of is that I'm not like most beings." He smiled. "I am certifiably unique."

"I've noticed." Her cheeks went pink and her smile returned, as bright as starlight in the darkness. His chest tightened and an unfamiliar warmth flowed through him. She had noticed *him*.

He belatedly realized he was staring and tore his gaze from hers. He really should be focused on their bigger problems right now – like the fact they were locked in what appeared to be an oblong metal box with only minimal comforts. If he could walk, it wouldn't take him more than maybe six long strides to travel from one end to the other, and it was maybe half that from the back wall to the makeshift door. Apart from a single, shelf-style bunk, the chair he sat in, and a boxy object that he guessed was a toilet based on the roll of toilet paper beside it, the cell was empty.

"Not exactly a five-star room, is it?" she asked as he finished looking around.

"Is there such a thing as a no-star rating? If so, we found it. Do you have any idea what this structure is? It doesn't look like it's part of a larger building."

"It isn't. I don't want to annoy the guards by wheeling you closer to the door so you can see for yourself, but we're in a large building, a warehouse, I think. This is a shipping container. A big steel box they pack full of goods to ship back and forth between countries." She pointed to one end. "That's the real door over there. The gate must be so they can keep an eye on us from out there."

"You don't think they're watching us remotely?"

"If they had that ability, they wouldn't have cut another hole in the container," she looked around thoughtfully, her brow furrowed as she toyed with a silver bracelet decorated with a variety of figures and beads. "Damn," she murmured in low, frustrated tones.

"More problems?"

She bent down so they were face to face, then raised her hand so her braceleted wrist was between them and whispered, "One of these charms is a tracking device. It should tell Megan exactly where to find us. Only, all this metal is probably blocking the signal."

"You wear such a thing all the time?" The concept shocked him. Even knowing that this world was dangerous, and that Lily's work took her to some of the most unstable areas, the idea that she had to carry that kind of security measure made his heart twist in his chest.

She nodded and lowered her wrist, but kept her voice to a hushed whisper, their faces so close together he could feel her breath on his cheek. "Megan gave one to each of us. Hanna's is part of her necklace." She straightened suddenly. "Hanna!"

Without another word she slipped over to the gate

and peeked out, using the wall to shield most of her body from view.

"What can you see?" he asked.

"Two guards. They're armed and standing between us and another shipping container on the other side of the warehouse." She bounced on her toes. "Oh! That one has two doors. I think that's where they must be holding Hanna and Jet."

"How far?"

Lily shook her head. "I'm really lousy at judging distances. Maybe thirty metres? The guards are spaced out in line with the ends of the shipping containers, facing each other."

"Better field of view that way. Interesting that there are only two of them. Do you see anyone else around?"

Lily peered around, then hissed in dismay and ducked behind the wall again, out of sight. "There's a group of men headed this way."

"Then you better put my hood back on. No sense antagonizing them."

Her eyes narrowed. "I don't want to. I want them to cut you loose, so you can be comfortable."

"They despise me. They're not going to care if I'm comfortable or not. Put the hood back on, Lily. They'll know you took it off, and I don't want you to be punished for your kindness."

"I hate this." Lily's expression was stormy, but she placed the hood over his head. Her fingers caressed the side of his neck, and the simple contact sent a flood of heat coursing through him.

He heard her move away and resented the need for her to leave him. The distance between them was necessary for her safety, though. Whatever happened, he would do all he could to protect her. He might not have a dragon's spirit, but he'd spent his entire life defending himself without the benefit of magic. He would keep Lily safe. No matter what the cost.

CHAPTER THREE

Putting the hood back on Vykor felt like a betrayal, but she did it. Not because she was afraid of the price she might pay for disobeying their captors' instructions, but because they were more likely to take out their anger on Vykor. He represented everything the Humanity First movement hated. She couldn't let that happen.

She knew what it was like to be a target of hate. She'd survived a childhood full of abuse, pain, and fear. If she could prevent them from going after Vykor, she would.

Heavy footsteps approached their cell. A lot of footsteps. She hadn't had time to do a headcount of the group coming their way, but it had to be at least six by the sound they made. She winced. The bigger the group, the uglier this confrontation could get.

She took a seat on the edge of the bunk, painfully aware of the cold that seeped up from the metal, through her skirt and the pitifully thin bit of padding that functioned as a mattress. When the footsteps stopped, she kept her head down, softening her body language as much as she could. Megan had told them often enough that if they were ever kidnapped, it was important not to be seen as a problem. Stay quiet. Make them see you as people, not bargaining chips, and don't rock the boat.

"You don't look happy to see me, Little Lil. Why is that?"

No-no-no-no.

"Johnny?"

Her half-brother smirked at her and gave a wave of his fingers. "Hey, little sister."

"Half-sister." She had to force out the words past the iron bands of dread that locked around her chest. What the hell was he doing here?

John laughed and stepped back while two other men unlocked the gate and wrestled it along its track. Once there was room, he strolled inside with his usual swagger. His dishwater-blond hair was longer, his frame stockier. He had the body of a grown man and not the youth he'd been the last time she'd seen him, more than fifteen years ago. He'd only been seventeen the day he was found guilty of murdering their father.

He looked harder now. Crueller, if that was possible. He stuck a hand into the pocket of his stained and well-worn jeans, his eyes gleaming with malice. "I wanted to see you and say thanks for all your help, Lily. You really came through for us."

Just like when they were kids. He was always

blaming her for things he'd done. Twisting the truth to suit him, making sure that everyone thought the best of him and the worst of her.

She sank into a swamp of futility, pulled down by the past until she thought she might drown in it. The fear. The pain. The constant need to guard every word and action. She didn't want to go back there. Didn't want to be that person.

Nothing Megan had taught her applied to their current situation. John wasn't some faceless captor in a foreign country. He was family, and nothing she did would ever make him see her as a person. He wasn't capable of that kind of empathy.

"I don't know what you're talking about," she said, forcing as much steel into her tone as she could manage. "If I were working with you, I'd hardly be in a cell right now, would I?"

John tut-tutted. "After what you did to me? I've got trust issues, little sister. Can you blame me for taking precautions?"

His men crowded behind him, and she could see the way their eyes gleamed with bloodlust and anticipation. One of them walked behind Vykor. She recognized him as the same man who'd cut her bonds earlier. When John nodded, the big man tore off the hood.

Vykor looked around as if dazed. "Who are you? Why are we here?"

John nodded again, and the man behind Vykor struck him sharply across the back of his head. When he raised his hand again, she saw he was wearing brass knuckles. *Crap.*

"Don't speak unless spoken to. Do you understand?" John's voice was smug.

Vykor nodded once.

"Good." Then John turned his attention back to Lily. "Like I was saying, I wanted to thank you." He held up a hand. Dangling from it was a necklace and pendant she recognized immediately. It was Hanna's. Even from here, she could tell the clasp was broken and the setting empty. The gem holding the tracker was gone. "We would have never known about the tracking device if you hadn't told us about it. All your updates were greatly appreciated, too. The entire movement owes you our thanks."

She balled her fists at her sides and got to her feet, determined to stand up to him for once. "You bastard! I would never help you do something like this!"

John crossed the cell and backhanded her so hard she staggered, filling her vision with dancing lights that made it impossible to see. She'd been stupid to defy him, even if it had distracted them from Vykor.

"Don't you touch her!" Vykor bellowed.

There was a crack, a meaty thud, and all hell broke loose. Someone slammed into her, knocking her into a wall. By the time her vision cleared, all she could see was a dogpile of John's men struggling to restrain Vykor. He'd managed to break one of the chair's arms off and was using it as a club against his captors.

"Stop it!" She threw herself into the fray, trying to shield him with her body.

There was a curse, someone grabbed her jacket and hauled her back. She kept fighting blindly, but whoever held her was too damned strong.

"Enough," John hissed, pulling her in front of him before twisting her right arm behind her back. He held it just short of the breaking point, and she went utterly still.

"Haven't forgotten everything Dad taught us, then. Good."

She was panting and it took a moment for her to find breath enough to speak. "Make them stop. Please make them stop hurting him."

"Not yet. My boys have some anger to work off."

She swallowed hard. "He's no good to you dead. You've been planning this for months, considering every detail. I know how you think. We're not already dead, so you've got plans for us."

"True. The extra alien was a surprise, but I can use him." He tightened his grip on her arm and pain shot through her. "And you."

Once she'd sworn she'd never let anyone have power over her again. It had been easy to make that promise when she felt safe, but she wasn't safe anymore. They were in trouble, and she only knew one way to get them out. She hung her head in defeat. "If you stop your men right now, I'll cooperate. Whatever you need me to do, I'll do."

"You were going to do it anyway, but convincing

you would take time I really don't have right now." He grunted. "Don't test me, Lily. You step out of line, there will be hell to pay."

"I know." She did know. All too well.

John's grip loosened and he raised his voice so the others could hear. "That's enough, men. We need it alive, for now."

There were muttered complaints and a few more blows landed before the others stepped back from Vykor. She expected to see him slumped in the chair, beaten half to death. She was stunned to see that wasn't the case. His face was bloodied and bruised, but nowhere near as bad as she expected. He sat defiantly in the chair, his gaze locked on John, and there was fury in his eyes.

He swiped the blood from his mouth with his free hand, bared his fangs, and uttered three terse words. "Let. Her. Go."

There were a dozen important things she should have been thinking about. The pain in her arm, the dangerous men crammed into the cell with them, or the fact her asshole half-sibling had somehow become the leader of a terrorist group and used her to ferret out information about her and her friends, but all she could do was stare in fascination at Vykor.

He had fangs. *Fangs.* That should not be getting her hot and bothered, but it was. She had to be losing her mind. He was sexy as hell, and after the beating he'd just taken, he was worried about *her*.

"You are in no position to make demands, freak," John's voice was as cold as a Winnipeg winter.

Aware that things could spiral out of control any second, she flashed the Romaki a weak smile. "I'm okay. Are you?"

Several of the men glowered at her, and there were angry mutters from all through the group.

"Alien lover."

"Bitch needs a night with a real man."

"Traitor."

"She needs to learn her place."

John snarled at his men. "Cool it. She's my blood, which means she's my responsibility. I'll deal with her. Anyone touches her, they answer to me. Got it?"

The mutters stopped.

"Good. All of you, out. I need a minute alone with my sister."

The men trooped out in silence, though they shot a few nasty looks her way as they left. Typical. John was back in her life for five minutes and he was already turning everyone against her.

He released her arm and shoved her away from him. "You like that thing so much? Maybe I should cut it loose so you two can talk. I'm sure it's got a lot of questions for you, Lil. How nice do you think that thing will be now it knows what you did?"

"He's not a thing." She managed to stop before she said anything more. If she angered him again, he'd only hurt them. If she stayed quiet, maybe he'd go away.

Then she could talk to Vykor – if he still wanted to talk to her now he'd heard what John had to say.

———

VYKOR ACHED FROM THE BEATING, but the thing that hurt the most was seeing the look of defeat and doubt in Lily's eyes.

"He's your brother?" he asked her.

"Half," she said, not meeting his gaze.

"And you helped him with all of this?"

She raised her head just enough to meet his gaze, then shook her head the slightest bit. "No."

"Okay then." He gave her a small smile that made his split lip start bleeding again, then looked at the male she'd called Johnny. "She answered my questions, and I've decided I still like her more than you."

The male sneered. "You aliens really are stupid. She's a fucking scorpion. The only thing you can trust her to do is betray you."

The arrogant male walked toward the door, then paused and looked back at Lily. "I thought maybe you'd be smarter this time. That you'd choose to stand with your family for once. I should have known better. Since you've made your choice, I've made mine. Whatever happens to the alien, happens to you." He paused and his smile twisting into something truly vicious. "And whatever happens to me, happens to both of you. So, you better hope that I get what I want out of this deal."

"What deal? I don't even know what you've got planned," she said, her voice still barely louder than a whisper.

I'm doing a prisoner exchange with your friends tomorrow morning. If anything goes wrong, you're the ones I'm going to make an example of. You're my insurance policy, little sister. For your sake, you should hope things go smoothly tomorrow."

He stalked out of the cell and two men hurried to slide the heavy gate closed behind him.

"He is such an asshole," Lily muttered, her voice tired and full of bitterness.

"Agreed. You sure you're related?" He'd always wanted siblings and a family, but seeing a glimpse into Lily's had him wondering if maybe he'd been better off alone.

She snorted. "We both got our father's eyes. He got all the asshole genes, though."

"He hurt you." Somehow, he'd make John pay for that.

"They hurt you, too. I'm so sorry. They have Hanna's tracker. They knew about our meeting. I don't know how, but this is all my fault. You must hate me." Tears gleamed in her eyes and she dashed them away with an angry swipe of her hand.

"I don't hate you." He nodded to her wrist. "If you were with them, they'd have taken your bracelet, too. And this cell was clearly intended for you. You're just as much a victim as the rest of us."

Hope flared in her eyes. "Are you always this logical?"

He cracked a smile as she asked him the same question he'd asked her earlier. "I'm a researcher. Thinking things through is an important part of the job." He shrugged one shoulder, trying to sound casual as he added a more personal confession. "I was always angry as a child. I resented my differences, the way I was treated. It was…disruptive. The priests taught me how to control my emotions and be more logical. I suspect they did it as much for themselves as for me. Angry children are noisy. Calm ones are not."

"I learned the same lessons, but for different reasons. Getting emotional made it too easy to react the wrong way, to make a mistake."

They really had a lot in common. It surprised him. "I heard your voice when you recognized your brother. You were shocked to see him. Logically, that meant you had no idea he was involved."

She heaved a sigh and nodded, finally relaxing a little. "I'm glad you saw through his lies. Most people don't." Then she cocked her head again and gifted him with a small but genuine smile. "But you're not like anyone else I've ever met."

"There's no one else like me in the whole galaxy." He reached out to her with his freed hand. "And I've never met anyone like you, either. You fought for me. Got hurt for me. No one's ever done that before."

She crossed the short distance between them and took his hand in hers, trying to loosen the knots that still held the arm of the chair to his forearm. "I'm used to getting hurt. Growing up, it was a daily occurrence."

He grasped her hand and held it tightly as a strange feeling of rightness thrummed through him. "Me, too."

Her eyes widened and she stared at their joined hands with surprise tinged with dismay. "What are you doing? I need to get these ropes off and get a look at your injuries. They hit you a lot, and at one of them was using knuckle dusters. You might have a concussion."

"I'll heal. I might not have a dragon's spirit, but I'm still Romaki. I heal quickly, and none of them did any lasting injury to me. As for what I'm doing, I'm not really sure."

He drew her hand to his mouth and kissed her fingers gently. She was trembling, and he wished he could draw her in close and offer her real comfort instead of this simple caress. He wanted her in his arms where he could keep her safe. She was too precious to allow anyone to hurt her again.

Only she wasn't his to protect. She wasn't his at all. He was acting like a *rux*-struck male and – *Frost and flame.*

He inhaled sharply, letting her scent fill his lungs. She smelled divine. Like a perfect blend of all his favourite things. Need ran through his veins like a drug. She *was* his. He knew it. But she couldn't be. He didn't have a dragon's spirit, so this couldn't be happening. Not to him.

"Why are you sniffing me?" Lily interrupted his

racing thoughts, tugging at her hand until he grudgingly released it.

"Sorry. I just… There's something going on here I don't understand."

She cradled the hand he'd kissed in her other hand, holding it close to her body. "That makes two of us."

He shook his head to clear it, then raised his gaze to hers, doing his best to bank the flames of lust that threatened to consume him. She'd never untie him if he didn't get himself under control. "I apologize. I shouldn't have touched you without your permission. If I promise not to do it again, will you help me get out of this chair?"

Lily gave him an odd look, then muttered. "Don't go making promises I might not want you to keep." Then her eyes widened. "Oh god! Please, forget I said that. I don't know what's wrong with me."

Vykor suspected he knew what was wrong with both of them, but he wasn't ready to say it out loud. Not until he was certain, and maybe not even then. Timing was everything, and this just didn't seem like a good time to mention that on top of being involved in a motor vehicle accident, a kidnapping, and an unpleasant family reunion, they might actually, somehow, be destined to be together forever.

His brain might be addled by the beginnings of the Romaki mating fever known as the rux, but he wasn't so far gone he thought Lily would take that news well. First, he needed to be sure what was happening. Then he'd find a way to tell her – somehow.

It didn't take long to get the ropes undone, and Vykor rose from the battered chair to stretch his bruised body. His head still ached from the blows he'd taken and his body was a mass of bruises, but nothing was broken or even strained. By morning he'd be fully healed.

Lily seemed okay, too. Her heavy jacket had likely cushioned some of the hits she'd taken, but she was favouring one arm. The one John had twisted behind her back.

"How's the arm?" he asked as he paced the length of their cell, checking out the gate with each pass he made. He couldn't see much, but after a few circuits he'd spotted the guards, the other shipping container, and the general layout of the building they were in. At least, what he could see if it.

"It's sore now and it'll be stiff tomorrow, but nothing's broken." She rolled her shoulder gingerly and winced. "I'd forgotten how much that hurt."

"Let me take a look at that." He had no formal medical training, but a lifetime of beatings had motivated him to find ways to help himself heal faster. One of the archivists he studied with had pointed him to writings on the ancient arts of energy healing, and he'd learned all he could. Some of them were known on Earth, too. He'd been trying to determine if they'd been brought by the Romaki visitors in the past or been discovered independently.

"I'm fine."

"Humour me, *razdi*."

"There's nothing you can do. Well, not unless you've got an ice pack in your pocket. Maybe some ibuprofen?"

"I'm afraid all I had in my pocket were some breath mints, but they took them, along with my phone, communicator, and my wallet."

"Same here." She uttered a rueful laugh. "If my digital farm animals starve to death because I couldn't log in to feed them, I'm going to be really unhappy."

He liked the way she laughed. Soft and warm, just like the rest of her. "I'd still like to help ease your discomfort, Lily. Please, let me."

She considered for a second, carefully eased out of her jacket, and set it on the bunk. She wore a light top beneath, the fabric patterned with subtle swirls of indigo blue and silver.

He moved behind her and raised a hand, then paused. "May I touch you?"

She went still. "You were serious about that whole 'not without my permission', thing?"

"I was."

Her shoulders drooped and she bowed her head, hiding her face. "I don't usually like being touched. But…" She exhaled in a rush." I trust you."

"I won't hurt you." He made the words into a vow, and something deep inside him resonated with the words. He'd never hurt her. If he was right, she was his mate. It shouldn't be possible, but it was getting more difficult to deny what was happening. Dragon spirit or no, somehow, he had found his *sadina*.

He laid his hand on her shoulder blade. She flinched away, and he whispered her name in soothing tones.

"Sorry. It's not usually this bad, but seeing John again, getting hurt. I'm a mess. I need to get my head on straight."

"Right now, all you need to do is stay still and let me fix you."

"I should be trying to help you, not the other way around. You're the one they beat up."

"I'll heal on my own." He'd been so concerned about Lily he'd forgotten about his own injuries. The cuts were already closing over, and in an hour or two the swelling would subside.

He performed a slow, gentle exploration of her shoulder, working down to her wrist. She was tense and wary at first, and he took extra care not to cause her any discomfort as he assessed the injury. He found heat, a little swelling, and more temptation than he'd ever experienced.

This close to her there was no escaping her scent, or the warmth of her skin beneath his fingers. Her body was lush, with full curves he wanted to explore at length. Her hair fascinated him, each curl a perfect spiral of pale gold.

He returned his hand to her shoulder, and this time she barely flinched at all. He did what he could to ease the injury, infusing intention and energy into every touch, and by the time he finished she seemed more relaxed, her energy flowing more easily.

"Thank you. Was that some kind of Romaki magic?"

She froze. "I'm sorry. I guess it couldn't be, but it felt like magic to me."

Her voice held no condemnation, but he felt the sting of shame anyway. If he was right about their fate, then she had been cheated. She deserved better than a freak like him. "No magic. An old technique I learned at the temple. Humans have several disciplines along the same lines."

"More proof that your people have visited Earth before?" she turned to face him, her eyes bright with curiosity.

"Maybe. I imagine it will take me years to gather all the evidence and verify it."

"You're going to stay here on Earth? Even after this?" She gestured around them to the cell.

"I am. I want to. I have no reason to go back to Romak. I like your world. While there are still some who see me as different, many don't seem to care. I'm more accepted here than I will ever be back on my planet."

Lily's face clouded. "Most humans are decent enough. Not like these idiotic Humanity First followers. The Pyrosians coming here was a blessing. They're no threat to us, and neither are the Romaki." She gestured beyond the cell door. "They're following my brother, for heaven's sake. He's not involved because he believes in the cause. He's here because it benefits him some way."

"Power?"

She nodded. "Or money, though based on what I've seen, they're barely keeping the lights on around here."

She looked out the door again, then uttered a soft gasp. "Cupcake?"

She was gone before he could ask what she was talking about, dropping to her knees by the gate, her hands held out through the bars. She whistled softly, and a massive shadow detached itself from the far wall and trotted toward them.

"What in the name of the Lady of Flame is that?"

"Cupcake, come here sweetie," Lily crooned to the approaching beast. It was some kind of canine, though he'd never seen one that big before. Its head was as broad as a shovel, and its fangs gleamed as the big creature came closer.

"Lily, do you think it's safe for you to be that close to that thing?"

She shot him a surprised look over her shoulder then turned back to the dog, her next words coming in a sing-song cadence. "Cupcake is not a thing. She's a good girl. Isn't she? Yes, she is."

The dog pressed her muzzle between the bars and started to wag her stumpy tail so hard her entire body moved. Her black eyes closed in bliss as Lily started rubbing her ears, and the dog leaned into the gate so hard Vykor heard the metal creak. Frost and flame, the animal was huge.

"Cupcake? Who named her that? And how do you know her?"

She continued petting the big, black beast and Vykor felt a pang of utterly irrational jealousy. "I named her. My brother called her Ravage, but then John got tossed into prison again and my mother agreed to take care of his puppy. I came over one day and discovered Cupcake had been left alone in mom's kitchen. She'd eaten an entire batch of cupcakes, papers and all. She even mangled the baking tin." She laughed. "After that, we started calling her Cupcake. By the time my brother was released, the name had stuck."

She went still. "Oh, damn. Mom. That has to be it."

"I'm sorry. Has to be what?"

Lily sighed, her voice weighed down with sadness. "She must be the one who told John everything. The tracker, our arrival. All of it."

He joined Lily near the door, though he stayed behind the wall, out of sight of anyone outside. "Why would she do that?"

"Because she doesn't see what John is. She never has. When she looks at him, all she sees is the boy who sacrificed his freedom to save us from a monster." Lily shuddered. "While all I see is another monster."

CHAPTER FOUR

LILY COULDN'T FIND it in her to be angry with her mother. The woman had never been a good judge of character. She believed John was as much a victim as they had been. She was always making excuses for him, all while encouraging Lily to allow her half-brother back into her life. There wasn't a snowball's chance in hell that would happen. John might have fooled her mother, but Lily knew better. Not all the scars she bore had been inflicted by their father. Her brother was just as vicious, and a great deal more cunning.

"He hurt you." There was an undertone of anger to Vykor's statement.

"Our father liked to take out his rage and frustration on all three of us. Until the day he killed our father, John only had one target. Me."

"He killed your father?"

She nodded. After so many retellings, the story had lost most of its impact for her. She recited the details as if she were talking about the weather. "John shot him in our kitchen while no one else was at home. He'd planned everything. The killing, how he'd get rid of the body and dispose of the murder weapon, all of it. But I came home early from school and found the body. I called the police before I knew who had done it…and John went to prison." She shrugged. "He still blames me."

"It was that bad at home?"

"It was bad, but we could have left. I wanted to go so badly, but I was too young to do it on my own, and mom was too scared to leave. I don't know why John stayed. It wasn't to protect us. I think he was too angry to go until he'd had his revenge."

"No one else knew? Why didn't anyone help you or your mother?"

"There were some people who knew, or at least suspected, but none of them did anything. Not while he was alive, anyway. They were all happy to testify at John's trial, though. Thanks to them, my brother got a lighter sentence. They thought they were saving him." She snorted. "None of them had any idea how dangerous he was, and none of them ever considered he wasn't the one that needed their protection."

Cupcake licked her fingers, and Vykor crouched beside Lily, offering her the comfort of his presence. She surprised herself by leaning into him, and a moment later his hand was at the base of her neck, his touch so gentle she barely flinched. She couldn't remember the last time that had happened. It was another reason her dating life was almost non-existent. Who wanted to be with someone who reacted to even the slightest touch? The only people she didn't react to were her mother and her friends, and even that had taken time.

"I want to protect you. I may not have magic, or the power of a dragon, but I can do that much," he said, his voice soft but determined.

"And if you do, they'll hurt you. Maybe even kill you." She shook her head. "I don't want that."

He reached up with his free hand to capture a curl, twining it around his finger. "And I don't want you hurt, either. You've already risked yourself for me. More than anyone else ever has. Why?"

She didn't look at him. "Because I'm not like my brother. I couldn't live with someone else's blood on my hands."

"And neither could I."

She didn't know what to say to that. So, she didn't say anything. Instead, she ruffled Cupcake's soft ears, eliciting a delighted grunt from the dog. She hadn't seen Cupcake in a few years, but she clearly remembered her.

"I hope John's taking good care of you, girl." She hated the idea of leaving the dog with someone with John's vicious nature. If she could have taken her, she would have, but she travelled so much and her apartment had a strict no pet policy. Besides, John would never have let her have Cupcake, and trying would have brought him back into her life. One thing today's encounter had made clear, she wasn't ready to take him on. She was still too afraid.

"Does he take you for walks? Hmmm?" *Walks*. The word bounced around her head for a long moment as an idea started to form. "Walks!"

"I think I'm missing some context here." Vykor's puzzlement was obvious, but there was a note of wry humour in his words.

"Sorry." She turned to face him. "My bracelet. Megan warned me it had a limited range, especially if we were deep underground or surrounded by metal." She waved around them excitedly. "But Cupcake needs to go outside at some point."

"And?" Vykor asked, then his eyes widened. "Walks!"

She stopped petting Cupcake and tried to undo her bracelet, but her fingers shook and she couldn't manage the clasp. She'd never met a guy who could follow her leaps in logic before. Even Hanna sometimes had to laughingly tell her to slow down and explain her thought process.

"Let me." Vykor's big hands wrapped around hers, he deftly undid the bracelet and then placed it in her hand.

She looked at Cupcake's collar, then the bit of silver jewellery. If she clipped the whole thing onto the collar, it would be noticed. How could she make this work?

"Could we separate the charm from the bracelet?" Vykor asked.

Once again, they were on the same wavelength. She

flashed Vykor a pleased smile, and his answering grin made her stomach flutter. It was getting increasingly difficult to remember that it was not a good time to go all mushy around the edges over a guy. Not even one as hot as him. "I think so."

A piercing whistle tore through the air and Cupcake flung her head up, out of Lily's reach.

"Ravage! Where the hell did you go? For fuck's sake, who let the dog out of my office?"

The dog dropped her head and whined softly as she got to her feet.

"Cupcake, come here for just a second. Come on, girl," she called softly, but she already knew the dog wouldn't come back to her. John was as unkind to the dog as he was to everyone else, and Cupcake had learned the same lesson she had as a girl – obedience was the best way to avoid pain.

She watched in frustration as Cupcake left, trotting by the pair of guards that stood watch, both of them wearing matching expressions of boredom and disinterest. They didn't so much as look at the dog as she passed.

"Damn it." She got to her feet, stuffed her bracelet into a pocket, then stared out the gate in frustration. "If they ever feed us, remind me to keep aside some treats so we can tempt Cupcake back here."

"You think she'll come back?" Vykor rose from the floor to stand beside her, close enough she could feel his body heat, but not quite close enough to touch.

"I hope so. She's starved for affection. She might come back just to get more pats, poor pup."

"Your brother doesn't deserve her."

"I know."

"When he goes to jail this time, will your mother take the dog again?"

"She usually does." Then the rest of what he said sank in. "You think he's going to jail for this?"

"I know he is." Vykor turned and looked down at her, his jaw set, eyes blazing. "We're going to survive this. Your friend Megan isn't the kind to give up, is she?"

"Megan is a freaking terminator. She'll never give up."

"Neither will my friend Karos. He's the first one of my kind to ever treat me like an equal. The first one I considered a true friend."

"He's a fire dragon, right? And the head of embassy security?"

"He's also a determined, dangerous male. He'll find us."

"They will." She clung to that thought, willing herself to believe it.

"And then, I'm going to ask your mother for ownership of Cupcake."

She blinked in surprise. "You will?"

Vykor's determined expression softened into a boyish smile. "Do you think she'd like living at the embassy? Plenty of beings around to pat her, and well… you could help me learn how to take care of her."

"I think she'd love it at the embassy." She found herself reaching out to squeeze Vykor's hand. "And I'd be happy to help you. Maybe I could even come to visit her sometimes?" She felt like an idiot for making the suggestion but before she could take it back, Vykor captured her hand in his, ignoring her reflexive attempt to pull away.

His smile widened until she could see his fangs, and her heart started to pound so fast she felt dizzy. "I'd like that."

"I'D LIKE THAT, TOO." He didn't even know if the embassy allowed pets, never mind one as massive as Cupcake, but he'd find a way to make it work. Not because he wanted the dog, exactly, but because he wanted to make Lily happy. He had no idea how to care for the animal, but he'd learn. For Lily, he'd do anything.

The thought shattered his reality, and when it reformed everything was different. His existence had always been a solitary one, a reality built for one. Not anymore. In that moment, he knew she was part of his life. Now, and forever.

"What's wrong?" Lily asked. "Is it your head? I bet it's your head. I knew you had a concussion." She led him to the shelf-like bunk and fussed at him until he sat down.

"I'm fine. No concussion."

She arched a delicate blonde brow and fixed him with an expression that would have made a charging k'taar change course. "Humour me."

"Of course, *razdi*."

She retrieved a small container of hand wipes from beside the toilet and then knelt on the bunk beside him. "May I clean up the blood and check your injuries?"

"Please."

She set to work carefully, her touch so gentle he barely felt it. "What does *razdi* mean?" she asked.

"The light of a star," he replied.

Her hands froze. "You're calling me starlight?"

"I am. Do you dislike it?"

"No! Uh, I mean I don't dislike it. It's pretty." She moved around behind him, her hands gently stroking through his hair as she checked him for lumps and cuts. "Why?"

"Because that's how I see you. A light in the darkness. Pure and constant."

The smallest of gasps escaped her. "That's... wow. That's probably the nicest thing anyone has ever said about me." She paused, then added. "But, don't stars twinkle? That's not very constant."

"They don't twinkle when you're in space."

"I didn't know that." She found the lump at the back of his head and he tensed as she brushed her fingers over it. "Maybe one day I'll see that for myself."

"You want to leave this planet?" He wanted to make his home here. What would he do if she wanted something else?

"Well, yes. Before the agreement with the Pyrosians is signed, Hanna wants to visit the planet. I'll go with her, of course. But unless there's a match for me on the Pyrosian's database, then I don't imagine I'll be staying."

"No," he growled, twisting around to look at her.

"No? No I can't go to Pyros? Why not?" Lily's eyes were wide and she pulled away from him, hands drawn in close to her chest.

It took longer than it should have to calm himself. It was likely the *rux*. He'd never expected to experience the mating fever, but he'd read the descriptions. A Romaki in the thrall of the *rux* was more primal, more in tune with the instincts of their dragon. *Which would be fine, but I don't have a flaming dragon. So, how is this happening?*

By the time he was in control again, Lily had her back to the wall and all the colour had left her face.

"That's not what I meant. I'm sorry. I just…" He ran a hand through his hair and fought to think clearly. "I was surprised you had applied for a Pyrosian mate."

"And your response to that was to tell me no?" She didn't move, but her expression was softer now, and her tone a little harder. He couldn't blame her.

"I'm sorry. It's been a strange day."

She nodded. "Agreed."

The silence stretched out for a long, painful moment. She didn't move her hands or relax her expression. He needed to fix this.

"I was jealous," he finally admitted.

Her mouth fell open. "What? Why?"

"Because I didn't like the idea of you going off to Pyros with someone else." He really hoped he was in the thrall of the *rux*. It was the only excuse he had for the insane words coming out of his mouth.

"Someone else." She repeated. "Someone not you?"

"Yes." He intended to stop speaking after that, but for some reason the words kept coming. "You belong with me, *razdi*. No one else."

"Oh." She gave him a shaky smile. "Is this a mating thing?"

Gods, she was clever. She'd figured it out almost as fast as he had. "I can't be sure, but I think so. I've never reacted to a female like this."

"Me either." She giggled softly. "I mean, I've never felt like this either. I can't stop thinking about how good it felt when you touched me before. And I got angry when they were hurting you. Angry enough I actually yelled at John."

"We want to protect each other. And ...other things."

Lily exhaled softly. "Those other things. It's getting hard to think about anything else. All I want is for you to touch me again."

"Is that a request?" his words came out with a rumbling note he'd never used before.

She turned bright red and nodded. "Yes."

He opened his arms to her, knowing it would be easier for her that way. "Come here."

She closed her eyes and moved toward him, almost

falling into his arms. He caught her and gathered her close, revelling in the moment. She hadn't rejected him. In fact, she'd come to him willingly. He was still angry at the Gods for abandoning him, but right now, that anger was tempered with gratitude for the female nestled against him. His mate. She was real, and he had found her.

Her hands moved over him, exploring. He followed her example, mirroring her actions with a gentle exploration of his own. He sank the fingers of one hand into her hair, letting them twine in her curls as he bowed his head to nuzzle her cheek with his. Her scent filled his lungs, as heady as the finest liquors and even more intoxicating.

Lily stirred. "What if this isn't what we think it is? What if it's just hormones and some kind of coping mechanism?"

"I almost hope it isn't the *rux*. Hormones would be a lot easier to deal with than the mating fever." And it would mean that she could decide for herself if this was what she wanted. If *he* was what she wanted.

Her hands stilled and her voice dropped to a whisper. "Because then you won't be mated to me?"

"No!" he barked the word and she stiffened then attempted to pull herself out of his arms. He didn't let her go. Flames, he was making a mess of this. Why did Jet think he had a future as a diplomat when he couldn't even manage a simple conversation?

Lily twisted in his grip, her movements more frantic. "Let me go."

"I'd rather not. I like holding you."

She stopped resisting and frowned up at him. "Has anyone ever told you that you're a very confusing man?"

"I'm actually a straightforward being. At least I was until today." He leaned in and touched his lips to her brow. "Until I met you."

She laughed a little and her tension eased. "I confuse you? You sure it's not just the fact we've been gassed and abducted, and beaten? Not to mention I still think you have a concussion. That would explain the confusion, too."

"I do not have a concussion," he stated firmly and pulled her closer. "What I have is a strong desire to kiss you."

"You already did that. But I'm happy for you to do it again."

"That was not a real kiss." He stared into her violet eyes, then bowed his head. "This is."

His mouth slanted across hers, drinking in her soft sigh of surrender as he did. Gods, she felt good. Soft and sweet, her curvy little body pressed against his, setting his blood on fire.

Her lips parted and she grabbed the front of his shirt, using it to pull herself up to meet his kiss with one of her own. Tongues touched and then tangled, and a raw moan of need vibrated against his chest. He didn't know which one of them made the sound, it could have been either of them, or both. Need coursed through him, and he speared his fingers into her hair, letting them tangle in the silken curls as he ravaged her mouth.

Jet suddenly called out from somewhere outside their cell and Vykor stopped so he could hear what was said.

"I know I'm not supposed to talk to you, and I promise to be sorry about it later, but is there any chance of getting a meal for the human females?" Jet said.

"If he's asking about food, then they must be relatively alright," Lily murmured with relief.

A gruff male voice called back. "Food for the ladies, yes. Food for you, no. We're not wasting food on no alien assholes."

"I'll share mine with you," Lily whispered.

"Thank you." Her generosity was as limitless as her kindness. He didn't understand why the Gods had abandoned him at birth only to reward him now, but if it meant keeping Lily, he'd accept their gift.

Hanna called out a thank you, and Lily's head snapped up. "She's smarter than I was."

"How so?"

"She's doing what we were taught and trying to make friends with the guards. Get them to see us as people instead of a means to an end. I should have done that. But when I saw John…"

"Your brother's presence changed things for you."

She snorted. "That's a heck of an understatement."

"I was trying to be diplomatic."

Lily's lips quirked up into a brief smile. "I think it's a bit late for that."

"Probably." He ran his knuckles down her cheek. "At least now we know they'll be coming to feed you, soon."

"Feed us," she corrected him.

"Best we don't mention that. They already think you're an alien sympathizer."

She smiled wider. "They called me an alien lover, not a sympathizer."

"Are you?" Something deep in his soul stirred as he waited for her answer.

Lily's cheeks heated and she lowered her gaze. "Not yet. But if I keep feeling the way I do now, who knows what might happen."

"If this is truly the *rux*, I know exactly what will happen. I just want you and me to be far from here when it does." He kissed her hard, every part of him aching for him to do more than kiss her. He wanted her naked and breathless beneath him, crying out his name as he claimed her. Until today, he'd never imagined he'd have a true mate. Until a few minutes ago, he didn't believe he'd ever be able to bond with a female, binding their souls together forever.

"Where will we go?" Lily asked when he finally broke their kiss.

"Somewhere we can be alone. It's a Romaki tradition to take our mates to a safe place far away from everyone else. For most, it's so their dragons can manifest without risk of destruction."

"And you really think I'm your mate?"

He nodded, capturing her chin in his hand so he could look into her eyes. "I do."

She smiled, but there was still a shadow of doubt in her eyes. "If we get out of here, then I guess we'll find out."

"We are getting out of here." He wasn't sure how it would happen, but he had to believe it would. They were both escaping this place, and then he'd take her far away and show her he could be a worthy mate, even without a dragon.

CHAPTER FIVE

THIS DAY KEPT GETTING WEIRDER. It was like she'd fallen into one of those daytime soap operas her mother loved. Abductions, danger, a sudden reunion with a dangerous family member, and now she was apparently mated to an alien. *Maybe I hit my head during the accident and I'm dreaming all this.* Except she knew she wasn't dreaming. If she was, her shoulder wouldn't ache, and she wouldn't be able to taste Vykor's blood on her lips. Kissing her had reopened the cut on his lip a little.

Without thinking, she swiped at the smear of blood beneath his lower lip, clearing it away with a fingertip. "You're bleeding again."

"Kissing you appears to be hazardous to my health. Although, it's not going to stop me from doing it again."

"I'm glad to hear it. We should probably stop for now, though. If our guards see us, they're likely to hurt you again." She suppressed a shiver at the memory of the beatings he'd already suffered.

He growled in frustration. "I know you're right. I don't like it, though." He scrubbed a hand through his hair, making it stand on end in spots. "I need to get you away from here."

"You can't." She didn't want to rub it in, but it was the truth.

He growled again, and there was something primal in the tone, an animalistic quality that hadn't been there before. "Not yet."

"We'll find a way. Right?" She forced herself to sound positive. She was tired of being afraid, but she couldn't seem to stop. It wasn't helpful, though. Fear and doubt wouldn't do either of them any good. She reached around him to retrieve her jacket from the foot of the bunk then fished her bracelet out of a pocket and held it up. "Speaking of which. We should get this ready."

"Which one is it?"

"The one that looks like an amethyst." She tapped a polished sphere of what appeared to be purple stone. "This one."

Vykor separated it from the bracelet with a few deft twists, then pocketed the charm. "When the time comes, you keep Cupcake happy and distracted, and I'll attach the charm to her collar."

"Good idea. Wait until I give you the signal, though. She's a sweetheart, but she can be leery of strangers."

And if they failed to get the charm attached this time, they might not get another chance. John said there was a prisoner exchange happening in the morning. That was their deadline. She doubted John could get the authorities to do anything that fast, and when he didn't get his way, he'd use the two of them to show his displeasure. They had to be gone before then.

Vykor reattached her bracelet, and tingles ran up her arm every time his fingers brushed her skin. For the first time in her life, she craved a man's touch. That fact alone made it easier for her to believe Vykor was her mate, even though it still seemed incredible to her. He'd told her he didn't have a dragon's spirit. From what she'd understood, both the Romaki and the Pyrosians mating fevers were triggered by some kind of mystical bond – magic. If Vykor couldn't access that magic, then how could he have a mate?

Her thoughts were fragmented, whirling around her head so fast it was like she'd dumped her mind into a blender.

Did he even want her? They barely knew each other. She'd signed up for the Pyrosian mating database and had been hoping for a match to an alien mate, but he hadn't expected to have a mate at all, never mind a human one. It was all happening so fast.

She blew out a breath and stood. She had too many questions and not nearly enough answers, but now wasn't the time to worry about it. She trusted him. More than she believed possible after so short a time.

She wanted him, badly. And if the kiss they'd shared was any indication, he wanted her, too. And they needed to work together if they had any chance of figuring out the rest of it. She'd tackle this just like she'd tackle a new project for Hanna – one step at a time.

Vykor stood, too, and neither of them spoke for a while. Their brief moment of passion had passed, at least for now. It wasn't safe for them to stay together for too long. She wasn't sure John had enough control over these men to prevent them from killing Vykor if they found out. Hell, she wasn't sure he'd stop them even if he could.

She wandered over to the doorway and peered out across the warehouse at the other shipping container. Hanna was over there. Lily gripped the chilled bars of the gate and wished she could talk to her right now. Did Hanna know who John was? Had he tried to convince her that Lily had betrayed her? What were they doing over there?

Her stomach rumbled, reminding her that it had been hours since she'd eaten. She always had a few snacks in her purse, but they'd taken that, along with everything else. At least they'd let her keep her coat. The handful of blankets on the bunk wouldn't do much to either of them warm tonight.

Her gaze swung back to Vykor, who paced the length of their cell in silence. Maybe later it would be dark enough for them to snuggle. It would be warmer that way. She grinned to herself. It was only practical, wasn't it?

Dinner arrived eventually, delivered by one of the men who'd stood guard for the last few hours. He didn't say anything, just slid a tray along a slot at the bottom of the gate and walked away again.

"Based on that meal, I'm going to have to change my rating to a negative number of stars," Vykor commented as he eyed the sparse selection. There was a peanut butter sandwich, some instant ramen soaking in barely warm water, a fruit cup and some bottles of water.

"Negative five stars. The server was hostile, the food uninspired and underwhelming." She tried to stir the soup with the solitary plastic spoon that had been on the tray. The ramen was still on the crunchy side and moved in a solid mass as she stirred it.

"And undercooked," Vykor noted, looking at the soup in dismay. "Or is it supposed to look like that?"

"If it was made with hot water, then the noodles would be soft. I'm afraid this is the best we're going to manage, though."

"I'm just glad they fed you." He walked over to the bunk where she'd set up the tray and took one of the water bottles from it.

"They fed *us*. You need to eat, too." She held out half of the sandwich to him.

He didn't take it. "There's not much there. I've been hungry before. It won't hurt me to miss a meal."

"It will hurt me to know you're hungry. Please, eat?"

He sat down beside her and accepted the sandwich

with a smile. "You are the kindest being I've ever met. Thank you."

She cracked open her bottle of water and took a long drink before answering. "I had a hard time of it growing up. Even after the trial, my mom and I still struggled. We were broke, with no family or real friends. We survived on the kindness of others. A landlord who never complained when the rent was late. Neighbours who made sure we didn't go hungry and brought over jackets and winter clothes their kids had outgrown so I had something to wear." She ate some of the sandwich. "Ever been to Toronto in the winter?"

"No. I've only been on this planet a few months. It is cold there?"

"Very." She cocked her head. "What are winters like where you're from?"

"It varies. As you might imagine, the Snow dragon clan likes the cold, while the Fire clan prefers more temperate weather. I was raised in the lands of the Snow Dragon Clan. Green in the growing seasons, and a place of terrible, cold beauty in winter." His eyes narrowed and his next words were edged in ice. "It matches the kind of beings that live there."

She met his gaze, reminding herself that the anger she saw there wasn't for her. It had taken her years to learn that lesson. Every raised word and angry gesture used to trigger her, but over the years she'd managed to slowly deprogram herself. She'd been so proud of herself. But all it had taken was one look at John and she had fallen into old habits. Somehow, she'd find the strength to stand up to him. She didn't want to be that scared little girl anymore.

THE MEAL WAS MEAGRE, but the company more than made up for it. Even at the embassy, Vykor had kept to himself most of the time. Everyone there had been warm and welcoming, but after a lifetime of being alone, he wasn't comfortable around large groups. He'd eaten his meals in his rooms, when he'd remember to eat at all. There was so much to read and learn about the humans and what part his species and the Pyrosians might have played in their development. There was no doubt that both species had been here before.

While they ate, he did something he'd never done before. He told Lily what he'd found, and what he thought it meant.

"Atlantis?" Lily exclaimed, her hands fluttering in excitement. "You think it was a real city?"

"More than that. I think it was one of the lost Pyrosian colony ships. Maybe they crash-landed. Maybe they decided to stay despite the fact the planet already had intelligent life. I'm going to request all future Pyrosian ships start doing deep scans of the oceans, starting with the most likely locations of the city of Atlantis."

"Because that city sank." Lily leaned forward, her enthusiasm and interest more gratifying than he could express. "You think they sank their ship. To what end?"

"Probably to hide the technology from the humans. Your species wasn't ready for it back then."

She snorted. "We're not ready for it now. I thought we'd have cured cancer and eliminated hunger by now. We should have. Instead, rich people are spending crazy amounts of money on luxury goods from other planets and nothing seems to be changing."

"It will come. When Prince Radek returned to my planet with his powers intact and a human mate at his side, it triggered a war. Here, change created so much fear and distrust that you and I are currently being held as hostages by a group whose greatest concern is that they won't get a date if the women of your world can get better offers from another species."

Her laughter rang off the walls and she clamped a hand over her mouth to muffle it, but her eyes still danced with mirth. Once she got herself under control again, she uncovered her mouth to reveal a broad smile. "You better not let them hear you say something like that…even if it is true."

"If they put half as much energy into trying to understand human females as they did organizing protests and bombings, they'd likely have found mates by now."

"Some of them, maybe. Most of them don't really want a mate the way you're thinking of them. They want someone to control. Someone they can lash out at when life doesn't go the way they want it to. Honestly, I hope none of them find women to date. They'll only hurt them."

"But they won't hurt you. I won't let that happen."

"*Protect.*" The thought came unbidden from the back of his mind, leaving him slightly unsettled. It hadn't been his thought. At least, he didn't think it was.

"We'll protect each other." Lily covered his hand with hers, the tender gesture soothing his anger like cool water over a flame.

He turned his hand over to intertwine their fingers, then leaned in to steal a kiss. She tasted sweeter than *veli* berries, and a hunger that had nothing to do with food tore through him, threatening to shred his control. He lost himself in their kiss, revelling in Lily's passionate response. She moaned softly, one hand lifting to stroke his face. He let go of her hand and wrapped his arms around her, lifting her onto his lap without breaking their kiss.

She settled onto his lap with another low moan, her soft weight pressing against his cock. The damned thing had been semi-erect since their first kiss, but now it was hard enough to rival steel. The *rux* was intensifying, and he didn't know how much longer he'd be able to fight its effects.

Lily stroked a hand up his chest, her fingers lighting on the buttons of his shirt. She toyed with them for a moment, then started undoing them until she could press her palm to bare skin.

"Should stop. Don't want to." She murmured between kisses, her voice low and husky.

"Have to." He tried to be rational, but the storm of

desire she stirred inside him was making it hard to remember why they should be stopping.

She huffed in frustration and pulled away just enough to break their kiss. "I'm losing my mind."

"Me too." He slid a hand up her flank to cup one generous breast in his hand. "But I'm not giving in to this madness here. It's too dangerous. When I claim you, my *sadina*, it will be somewhere safe, warm, and private."

"That's a pretty word. What's it mean?"

"Mate. You are my *sadina*."

"I like that better than mate. It sounds..." her hands fluttered between them. "It sounds proper, somehow. Is there a word for what you are to me?"

"Sodono."

She smiled, then repeated it carefully. "*Sodono*. I like that, too."

The way she said it made his heart gallop and his blood roar in his ears. It took him a moment to realize it wasn't a rush of blood he was hearing. It was something else. But what?

"Vykor? What is it? Every now and then you stare off into space, like you're listening to something I can't hear."

"I'm listening for Cupcake. I should be able to hear her claws on the floor." It wasn't a complete lie. He had been listening for the dog. It also sounded better than admitting he was listening to a weird noise only he could hear.

"You can hear her toenails click? Seriously?"

It was one of the many reasons he enjoyed living on Earth. Here, he was considered exceptional, his senses, healing ability and strength above average. No one could fly, either. The only time he saw a dragon overhead was when Karos stretched his wings. "I can."

"Any sign of her?"

"Not yet."

"Damn. I was hoping we could get the charm attached before someone took Cupcake out for her nighttime walk. It's got to be getting late by now."

As if in confirmation, the lights outside started going out, bank by bank. They rose from the bunk, untangling themselves as they went, and walked over to the cell door. There was enough light they could see the guards, and a few offices were still lit, but most of the warehouse was dark and quiet. A faint light came from the shipping container across from them, and a silhouette stood by the bars of one door. Jet, he guessed by its size.

The shadow vanished before he could do more than raise a hand to wave and he dropped it again before the guards noticed the movement. The last thing they needed was to attract unwanted attention.

Lily wandered back to the bunk and started tidying up the remains of their meal, stacking everything onto the tray, then carrying it back to the gate and sliding it through the slot in the bottom.

She shivered as she stood, and he moved out of sight to wrap an arm around her shoulders. "You should put your coat back on."

She leaned into his side. "I like this better. You're warmer than any jacket."

They stood in companionable silence for a while, just holding each other. One day soon, he wanted to hold her like this as they stood under a starry sky, or watching a sunset somewhere. Alone. At peace. Someplace he could strip her out of her clothes and claim her as his mate.

His cock twitched, his balls aching at the erotic thoughts that raced through his mind. He wanted to sink his fangs into her throat and taste her as he slid into the soft heat of her body. Wanted to feel their souls entwine, connecting them forever. He'd never be alone again.

A door slammed shut somewhere in the dim shadows, and the click of toenails on concrete caught his attention. "Cupcake's out there."

"Quick. Turn off the light so no one can see us. The tray's already out, maybe she'll come by to mooch for scraps."

He tapped the simple, battery powered disc that was their only source of light, and the cell went dark. He could still see Lily, though. She was a shadow by the doors, already crouched on the floor, facing outward.

"Come on Cupcake. I know you can smell the food. Come on, girl."

They'd left a bit of the broth in the bottom of the cup, and she had a piece of the sandwich stashed in her pocket. She'd been confident it would work, and as the sound grew louder, Vykor grinned. His clever little *sadina* had been right.

The massive animal moved into sight gradually, as if the shadows had come together to form her body. She grumbled a greeting, wagging as Lily crooned to her, holding out the soup container. She buried her muzzle into it, and Vykor hurried over to join them, the charm already in his hand.

"Cupcake, this is Vykor. He's a friend." She glanced over and nodded, then said in the same soft voice. "Move slowly, give her a second to get used to you. If she growls, don't pull away, just stay still a moment."

"If she bites me, are you going to kiss it better?" Now he was this close to the dog, he wasn't sure this was such a good idea. The dog's teeth were big enough to do some damage.

"She's not going to bite you. She's a good girl. Right, Cupcake?" She scrunched the dog's ears and she leaned into her hand, groaning in delight.

Vykor eased his hand through the bars, but the dog ignored him. Lily gave her the bit of bread and peanut butter while Vykor used the distraction to slip his other hand through the bars. He held the dog's collar in one hand and managed to attach the charm to a metal ring that already held a flat metal disc. He positioned the charm behind it, then moved his hand to stroke the top of Cupcake's broad head. "All done."

"She likes you." Lily guided his hand to one of the dog's ears. "Rub right there and you'll have a friend for life."

He did as she said and Cupcake leaned what felt like a half-tonne of weight against his hand, grunting and growling in pleasure.

Lily giggled. "I now pronounce you man and dog."

"If I rub your ears will you be mine forever, too?" He didn't know where the words came from, but whatever part of his brain was doing the talking really needed to shut up…or come up with some better lines.

"If we're really mates, it won't matter what you do. I'll be bound to you forever, right?"

He let go of Cupcake and turned to Lily, taking her by the hands and drawing her away from the door, out of sight of the guards. "You are my *sadina*. I know you are. That means you are mine to cherish and protect for the rest of our lives. Nothing in the galaxy will be more important to me."

"How can you be sure? I'm sorry, Vykor, but you don't have a dragon's spirit, so how is any of this possible?" Her hands moved within his as if she was trying to gesture with them, but he didn't let go.

Staring down at her in the dim light, the truth struck him like a comet. She really was his, and he would never, ever let her go. "Dragon or not, you're my mate. Maybe he's asleep, or maybe I don't have one at all. I don't have the answers. I just know that when I look at you, I see my future."

"You think he's asleep? Is that possible?"

"I don't know." He placed one of her hands on his chest, over his heart. "But if there is anyone in the world that can call my dragon, it would be you, my *sadina*."

"You want me to call him?"

"What harm could it do?"

She furrowed her brow, then nodded. "Good point." She cleared her throat and spoke again. "Hey, dragon? If you can hear me, we really need you right now. Until now, you've left Vykor to fight all his battles alone. Don't you think it's time you stepped up?"

He held his breath for one second, then two, then three. Nothing happened. No voice. No magic. No difference.

"Did it work?" she asked.

"No."

She sighed. "Well, it was worth a try. But I think I'm kind of relieved. I mean, I know Vykor, the man standing in front of me right now. I don't know anything about dragons."

He gave her a rueful smile. "It seems that isn't going to be an issue for either of us."

"But we are mates, right? I mean, we wouldn't feel this way if we weren't."

"We are mates. That much I am sure of."

She nodded. "If your dragon isn't going to make an appearance and get us out of here, then I guess we'll just have to wait a little longer to be together. It's getting difficult to think about anything else. I don't know how much longer I can do this, Vykor."

He folded her into his arms, every part of him hard

and aching with need. "Just a little longer, *razdi*. Then we can give in to the madness."

She trembled and nestled closer to him. "Alright, my mate. I'll wait."

She'd called him her mate again. She believed they were destined for each other. Nothing had ever sounded so good.

CHAPTER SIX

Lily didn't sleep much. How could she, when she had more than six feet of sexy, aroused alien pressed against her? They shared the bunk as best they could, but the limited space meant that Vykor was on the thin mattress, while she sprawled on top of him. They slept in their clothes, huddling beneath their jackets and the one meager blanket left for them. Their shared body heat helped stave off the worst of the chill, though they were both too far gone into the *rux* to really pay attention to anything but each other.

Every kiss raised her body temperature another degree, and when he slipped his hands beneath her blouse to stroke bare skin, she felt like she might burst into flames. She was drunk on desire, and it took every ounce of willpower she had left not to tear off her clothes and let him take her. Not even the thought of letting him see her scars gave her pause, which was a testament to how powerful the *rux* had become. She hid the evidence of her abuse from everyone, but she wouldn't do that with Vykor. He'd already seen what her past looked like, seen how afraid she could be, and hadn't turned away.

She dozed fitfully over the course of the night, too keyed up to rest for more than a few minutes at a time. Lying together like this was a risk and they both knew it, but it was warmer this way, and as hard as it was to touch him without doing more, it was easier than being away from him. She needed to feel him, to stay connected no matter what.

They were on their feet seconds after the lights came on in the warehouse. Vykor moved to the doorway, peering out as men started calling out to each other in greeting. He guarded the door while she used the toilet, mortified at the necessity to do so in front of him.

"Looks like they're bringing food to Hanna and Jet," he reported after a few minutes.

"Nothing for us?" She asked as she used one of the hand wipes to clean off her hands, then used several more to tidy herself up as much as she could. Her hair was a chaotic tumble of curls, her clothes were rumpled, and she didn't have a stitch of makeup left, but at least she felt a little cleaner.

"Doesn't look like it."

She stretched and wandered over to join him. "When we get out of here, we're going to find a nice restaurant and order everything on the menu, along with about a dozen cups of coffee. I would kill for a latte right now."

"If I could, I'd conjure you everything you could wish for. A feast fit for a queen, as well as a sanctuary to shelter us during the *rux*."

"You don't have to do anything like that. All I really need is a hotel with room service. Ooh, and maybe one of those decadent jacuzzi tubs."

He placed his hand on the small of her back, his fingers moving in slow, concentric circles that were so distracting she almost forgot what they were talking about. "I will take you into the mountains. Somewhere we can be alone. It's a tradition among my species. Though we'll need some help getting there."

"I don't care where we go, as long as we get to be alone, soon."

"Agreed."

"If you had magic, would you really make me a feast? Do you know how to do that?" She raised a hand and moved it around like she was waving a magic wand. "Abracadabra, Harry Potter, Poof!"

He chuckled. "No need for a wand. As a boy, I memorized and practiced all sorts of spells and incantations, both Fire and Snow magic. I desperately hoped that the priests were wrong. I had to do it in secret, of course."

"What? Why? Didn't the priests want you to be ready in case your dragon appeared?"

He shook his head, lips thinned, eyes hardening for a brief second. "They had made up their minds already. The kinder ones thought of me as one the Gods had somehow overlooked. A forgotten child they should pray for. There were others that thought I was proof the Gods were displeased with my species, or that I was being punished for some terrible transgression by my parents. They believed that by punishing me, they were doing the Gods' work."

A surge of anger, raw and powerful, burned away the fog of lust that clouded her senses for a moment. "It's a good thing they live on another planet, or I'd kick their butts for what they did to you!"

His anger faded instantly and he looked down at her with amusement tinged with surprise. "You actually mean that."

"Of course I mean it. Those priests were assholes." She pointed out the gate to the grim-faced guards. "Just like those guys. Arrogant, heartless jerks who spend their whole lives lashing out at anyone or anything that doesn't fit into their limited worldview."

Vykor chuckled, stepped behind the shelter of the wall, then tugged her into his arms. "My little *razdi*. How I adore you."

Then he kissed her with bruising intensity, crushing her against him as his kiss stole her breath, then her mind. She was so caught up in the kiss it took her a second to really register the booming roar that shook the walls of their cell. It wasn't until the second roar tore through the air that she realized Vykor had lifted his head and was staring at the ceiling, grinning so broadly his fangs showed.

"What is that noise?" she asked.

"Karos," Vykor replied, still grinning. "They found us."

She stepped away from Vykor to peek through the bars. The warehouse was in chaos. Men shouted as they ran for the doors. They were all armed and angry, but they weren't working together. Instead they bunched up in front of the doorway, weapons raised as they yelled and shoved at each other.

The only ones acting deliberately walked together, and they were heading straight for them. In the middle of the group was her half-brother, and he wore an expression that chilled her soul.

"We're in trouble." She stepped out of sight and tipped her head toward the door. "John and a handful of his men are heading this way."

Vykor cursed and leaned over her to look for himself. "They're wearing tactical armour."

"Probably spent their whole operating budget on it. We know they didn't spend it on the décor around here." She didn't know why she was making jokes at the moment. A reaction to the fear, maybe?

The air was full of the sound of gunfire and panic, punctuated by the bellows of an enraged dragon that was invariably followed by terrified screaming. Explosions boomed, shots rang out, and Lily was almost grateful she was safe inside. Only she wasn't really safe.

Vykor backed away from the door, drawing her behind him as he went. She wouldn't stay there, though. He was in as much danger as she was. Maybe more.

John appeared at the gate. "Both of you stand by the bunk. If you move, my men will shoot you. Understand?"

"Got it," she replied, amazed at how steady her voice sounded.

Two men hauled the gate open and then two more stepped into the cell. One had his weapon trained on Vykor, the other was aiming at her. Adrenaline surged through her veins, filling her with an almost irresistible urge to do *something*.

John reappeared. "New plan. You and the freak are coming with us."

She stepped in front of Vykor and glared at her brother. "He's not a freak!"

"Don't fucking start, Lily. You were never smart enough to know when to shut the hell up. Now, get over here and don't do anything stupid. I've already killed one member of this family. Don't think I won't do it again."

"She stays here," Vykor said.

"The hell she does. There are two fucking dragons out there right now, along with a bunch of alien bastards hurling fireballs. You two are my ticket out of here. Now both of you shut up and get over here." John snapped his fingers and pointed to the ground in front of him, and something inside of Lily cracked wide open, spilling out a torrent of fear, loathing, and pain.

"No! This is insane. You're insane. I'm not going

anywhere with you." She hated the way her voice quavered and cracked. Why couldn't she be stronger than this?

"Leave her." Vykor's voice was louder now. "I'll go, but only if you leave her here where it's safe. You only need one hostage. Take me."

"I don't have time to fuck around." John took two steps and grabbed her by the wrist, yanking her toward him. She screamed and stumbled into him, accidentally kicking him as she tried to regain her balance.

"Bitch!" John snarled, and there was a flash of metal, followed by a blinding flash of light and a terrible sound that deafened her. Something slammed into her like an invisible fist, and she crumpled to the ground. Agony tore through her but she didn't even have the breath to scream as a terrible darkness rose up and swallowed her whole. *No! I don't want to die. I want to stay with Vykor.*

THE BASTARD SHOT LILY.

Vykor bellowed, giving voice to his fury and grief. He charged at John, but as he ran another presence roared to life inside him, taking over his mind and changing his body into something else. Something new. A dragon.

"Protect!"

The beast was dominant, too full of rage and pain for him to control, but he didn't care. All that mattered was Lily. He wrapped her in a protective bubble of magic, lifting her onto his back even before the transformation was complete. He shielded her with his wings, protecting her from the shredding metal of the container as he tore through it, and from the bullets that bounced off his skin as the men with John opened fire.

Fire. His dragon roared in agreement. They stepped out of the shattered remains of the steel shell that had been their prison, then turned and sent a blast of white-hot fire at the wreckage. Within seconds, the area was nothing but molten metal and ash, including the men who had hurt his *sadina.*

"*We protect,*" the dragon rumbled inside his mind.

"*You were too slow. We failed,*" Vykor snarled. "*Where were you?*"

"*Trapped. Your walls. Your prison.*"

He didn't understand. What walls?

Hanna's voice, shrill with worry, cut through the air. "Hey, dragon! What the hell did you do to my friend?"

The human female stood beside Jet. They both looked tiny to him now. He could swat them away with a single swipe of his tail.

"*No,*" he told the dragon. "*We don't hurt our friends.*"

He raised his head, the beast snorting in irritation at Hanna's question – and possibly Vykor's attempt to restrain him. He spread his wings so they could see Lily draped across his back.

"*Vykor, welcome to the skies,*" Karos' voice sounded inside his mind, startling him.

"Brother!" his dragon responded to Karos before he could.

"It is safe to leave. Are you all unhurt?" Karos asked.

"Lily is hurt."

If it was safe to leave, then it was time to get Lily out of here.

"Protect," his dragon agreed, and once again the creature took control, turning his head to face the wall of the warehouse. A blast of cold flowed from his jaws, coating everything it touched with a thick layer of frost. The crystalline sound of ice cracking filled the air, and he spun, slamming his tail against the wall. It gave way beneath the force of the blow, and he took a moment to marvel at his own strength. *This* was why his people feared the destructive power of an uncontrolled dragon.

He moved through the hole he'd made, careful to keep Lily sheltered from the shattered edges of the gap and the waves of cold that poured off the rubble. Once outside the scents of death grew stronger. He hadn't taken an active part in the war that had almost destroyed the Romaki civilization, but he'd been close enough to some of the battles to remember the smell. Now his senses were enhanced, the odours hit him even harder. Fire, gun smoke, blood, and death filled his senses, a sickening miasma he'd never forget.

Two dragons hurtled toward them, the smaller one wobbling slightly as it approached. It struck the ground hard, lost its balance, and went crashing into a nearby warehouse with an impact that shook the ground beneath his feet.

"My mate is unused to flying," Karos explained through their link, a trace of amusement and pride in his words.

"Mate?" It would seem the Gods were up to more than their usual mayhem.

"We have much to discuss." There was a pause before Karos added. *"Have you seen your dragon form, yet?"*

"No." He swung his head around to look at himself, and nearly stumbled over his own feet in shock. He was neither red, nor blue. By Solun's frosty beard, he was purple!

TIME FLEW by in a frantic blur for a time. He'd shifted forms and the power of the dragon had receded. The creature still paced in the back of his mind - a barely restrained force fuelled by need and worry for their mate.

He hadn't thought to dress after the shift, but Karos had taken care of it, wrapping him and Lily in blankets as Vykor carried her to safety.

Pyrosian medics worked on Lily, speaking in a shorthand he didn't understand. He recognized the tone beneath the words, though. They were worried.

He held fast to her hand, refusing to be parted from her. He should have done more to protect her. Gods, he should have claimed her last night and hoped that even without the manifestation of his dragon, the claiming would have been enough to make her Romaki.

Guilt tore through him, along with growing anger. The Gods had finally gifted him with a dragon's spirit. Why now? And why hadn't it come in time to protect the female they'd chosen for him? Was he still being punished?

He gripped her hand tighter. He couldn't lose her. If the Pyrosians couldn't save her, he'd do it himself, even if he didn't have her permission.

Cupcake leaned against his legs and whined softly, as if she understood Vykor's thoughts. The big dog had appeared just as Vykor had shifted forms and hadn't left his side since.

"She's going to be okay, girl. I'll make sure of it." He reached down to rub one of Cupcake's ears.

"That animal really shouldn't be here," someone commented sourly.

Vykor glowered at the male. "She's not going anywhere, and neither am I. Lily is my mate. Do you understand?"

The male's gold eyes widened in sudden understanding. "I see. Just…try to stay out of our way, please. But don't let go. She needs to know you're here."

He nodded. "Can you heal her?"

The medic started to nod, then stopped. "I honestly don't know. Her injuries are very serious." He looked thoughtful for a moment, then added, "Your species has tremendous healing powers. Given her condition, I'm assuming you haven't claimed her, yet?"

"No. But if you can't save her, I will." *Even if she never forgave him for it.*

Consent was an integral part of Romaki matings. The Gods might be the ones to make the matches, but it was important that everyone was in agreement before things progressed. If he claimed Lily, he'd be doing more than changing her marital status without permission. He'd be changing her identity. She wouldn't be human any longer. She'd be Romaki, subject to the laws and pressures of a species she'd never known, and one he didn't want any part of.

CHAPTER SEVEN

It felt like an eternity passed as he stood by her, but it couldn't have been more than a few minutes. The medical staff worked frantically, but in the end, they backed away from the table and looked at him, their expressions grim. "If we were back at the embassy we could have done more, but we're not, and she's too weak to survive the journey. If you think you can save her, do it now."

"*Ours. Protect. Claim!*" his dragon sounded almost frantic.

"*Yes.*" He bent over her still, broken form, cradling her head in one arm. Her too-pale face was spattered with blood, and he took a moment to kiss her brow. "Forgive me, *sadina*. But I cannot live without you."

Then he shifted her in his arms, her head falling to one side, her throat exposed. He summoned his dragon and they claimed her together, his fangs tingling as they sank into her flesh. Magic – his magic – flowed into her, a dizzying sensation that cumulated in one unforgettable moment when their souls bonded, tying them together for the rest of their lives.

He stayed where he was, holding her to him as he watched her face for signs of life. "Come back to me, Lily. Your brother can't hurt you anymore. I saw to that. It's time to wake up. You're stronger than he ever was, and I've made you stronger, still. Wake up, my *razdi*. I need you."

She stirred, and the machines monitoring her life signs started showing green lights instead of red. One by one the alarms stopped. He didn't look away from her face. He didn't need to see the wound close over to know what was happening, he could feel it. She was healing.

All around them beings sighed with relief tinged with wonder. The Pyrosians had magic of their own, but it was nothing like the power wielded by the Romaki.

Her eyes fluttered open slowly, and then she smiled. It was a tiny twist of her lips, but to him, it was the most beautiful smile he'd ever seen.

"Hi," her voice wasn't more than a rusty croak.

"Hello, *razdi*. Welcome back."

Beside them, Cupcake gave a happy bark, standing on her hind legs, paws on the stretcher so she could see Lily.

"We're safe?"

"We are. All three of us."

"And I'm not dead. That's a definite plus." She lifted

her head and stared down at her now uninjured body. "But I was shot, right? I didn't imagine that asshole shooting me, or the universe of ouch that came with it?"

"He shot you. I killed him. He won't hurt you ever again." He didn't try to keep the smugness out of his words. Killing John had been a highlight in his day.

"I remember bits of it." She frowned. "I got shot. Passed out. But then later, I was up in the air. On a… dragon?" Her violet eyes rounded in surprise. "You manifested your dragon!"

"Too slowly to protect you. I'm sorry about that." He'd failed her twice. If he'd protected her the first time, he wouldn't have been forced to convert her without consent.

"But he's no threat now. He's really dead?"

"Very." The seconds after his transformation weren't very clear, but he had a vague recollection of stomping John into paste. The male was dead even before he'd melted their prison to slag.

"So, the bastard shot me. But I'm not shot now?" She looked around at the medical equipment and the Pyrosians, who were all stepping back to give them as much privacy as they could. "How?"

He told her the truth, hoping that somehow, she'd forgive him. "When the medics couldn't save you, I did. I'm not proud of what I did. It's not the way it should be done. I bound our souls together without permission. I stole a precious moment that should have been shared, but I had to do it. I couldn't live without you, *sadina*."

She stared up at him, her eyes wide with understanding. "You claimed me so I could heal."

"I did. Can you forgive me? I will make it up to you however you wish. Anything you desire. You deserved better."

She laughed, sweet, silvery peals of delight that swept away his doubts and worries like a soft spring rain cleared away the last snows of winter. "Forgive you for what? For saving my life? For making me into a dragon? I am a dragon, right? If you're one, then I must be. I told you the Gods didn't abandon you. Ha! Take that, nasty priests!"

She pumped a fist in the air, then froze, her gaze locked on her bare arm. "I uh… don't appear to be wearing much clothing."

"Neither of us are." He hadn't even noticed, but he was still wearing nothing but the blanket Karos had conjured for him.

"Can you fix that?" She waved one hand in the air. "You know, bitty-bobbity-poof?"

Frost and Flame, he adored her. Barely recovered from injuries that could have ended her life, and she was already joking and laughing.

He gestured at her gore-streaked body "Would you like to clean up, first?"

"Ew! Yes. I'm a mess."

"I think you are amazing."

She snorted and scrubbed a hand over her stomach. "Yeah, an amazing mess. This is not the way I imagined you'd be seeing me naked for the first time."

Heat streaked through him, and the fires of the *rux* roared back to life in a heartbeat.

"No? What did you imagine?"

"Less blood, for one thing. And no audience."

Audience. Right. He fought through the lust fogging his brain. Now was not the time to lose control. He'd have her alone soon, but this wasn't the time or place. He'd take her to the mountains, love her, and then they could both learn all they could about their new natures.

"We can help you get cleaned up." A Pyrosian female offered. He noted that all of the males had left the immediate area. Wise of them. Now that the danger had passed, he wouldn't tolerate another male near Lily.

"*Ours,*" his dragon stated.

"*We're going to have to work on your vocabulary. Maybe try more than one word at a time?*"

The beast replied with a sense of pure disdain. "*Later. Now we claim.*"

"*Soon,*" he retorted.

This time the reply was accompanied by a trace of amusement. "*Also one word.*"

Wonderful. After years of waiting, he'd finally manifested a dragon – and he was already giving him attitude.

LILY KNEW she should be more concerned about things. Her friends, her near-death experience, her new status as a married – or mated – woman, the fact she'd changed freaking species while she was unconscious. Not to mention that while she'd sort of wrapped her head around the fact she was mated to Vykor, now she had to deal with the fact he was a freaking dragon! Any or all of those items really deserved her attention, but she couldn't focus on any of it. Not for long.

Vykor commanded all of her attention, and she was enjoying herself too much to fight it. He'd stayed by her side as she cleaned herself up with some help from a Pyrosian woman with the most beautiful golden eyes. Once she felt close to normal, he'd created clothing for them both. It was sumptuously soft, almost like velvet. The pants were loose-fitting but comfortable, and the shirt was almost bohemian in style, long and flowing. She loved it, especially the colour – violet.

"To match your eyes," he'd told her as he'd lifted her into his arms. His outfit was similar to hers, but he'd chosen midnight blue for himself. They both wore slip-on type boots with warm fur lining. He hadn't conjured underwear for her, and the luxurious fabric caressed her bare skin with every step she took.

She could see the changes in him already. He was more confident, his smile broader, his movements bolder. He was harder, too. Like a blade that had been forged in the hottest of flames. He was still her Vykor, though. Thoughtful, tender, and attentive. At least, she hoped he was.

"You ready to see the others?" he asked while they

were still alone. "If it's too much, I can take you away right now and we'll talk to them later."

"I want to see them. I need to. I won't believe they're alright until I see it for myself. Plus, I need to make sure they know I wasn't part of this." That was the part she dreaded the most. What if they thought she'd betrayed their trust? John was one of the most convincing liars she'd ever known. Plus, they were both mated now. What if their mates didn't believe she was innocent? Karos and Jet didn't know her, and they had every reason to suspect she was in on it.

"They're your friends. You should have seen how worried they were about you while you were unconscious. Believe me, they know you had no part in what happened. We all know better than that." He looked down. "Right girl?"

Cupcake wagged enthusiastically. The dog was as smitten with Vykor as she was.

"Then let's do this."

He carried her around the corner, and she spotted her friends. Both of them started running toward her, beaming and calling her name.

Relief hit her and she waved like mad. "I'm okay, it was merely a flesh wound!" Monty Python's Holy Grail was one of Hanna's favourite movies and she knew they'd get the joke.

They crowded around her, both of them talking and hugging her at once, which wasn't easy given Vykor still held her.

"What happened?" Megan's query was the first clear question she heard. "Who hurt you?"

The question triggered a surge of emotion far stronger than she'd been expecting, blasting through the fog of lust and contentment that had shielded her until now. Shame, sadness, and anger flowed out of her along with a torrent of tears. ""It was John. He did this. I'm so sorry, Hanna. I didn't know. I swear, I didn't know anything about this. I didn't even know he was part of this stupid group until he walked into my cell."

Hanna took her hand and squeezed it tight. "I know. John used you."

"I didn't tell him a thing!" Lily's voice rose. "I told my mom about your necklace because I thought it was a cool gizmo. I never told her I had one, too. I didn't want her to worry about why I might need such a thing. I never thought she'd tell anyone. This is all my fault. I'm so sorry."

Megan took her other hand and gripped it just as tightly as Hanna was. "You weren't the one who gassed us, or who told your asshole brother we were coming. Kyle did that. But you did find a way to get your tracker outside the walls so we could find you. How'd you do that, anyway?"

"Cupcake. She's my brother's dog. I managed to slip my tracker onto her collar. I hoped that when they took her for a walk, you'd get the signal." She beamed. "It worked, didn't it?"

"It did. Good thinking." Megan grinned back at her, and she knew that everything would be alright. Things might have changed for all of them, but Megan and Hanna were still her friends.

A few minutes later her friend's mates came over to join them, both males staking very public claims to their women. Jet had his arm across Hanna's shoulders, and the big redheaded Romaki stood behind Megan with his arms wrapped around her waist. It didn't take long for her to realize that she wasn't the only one distracted by the touch of her mate. It made sense—both species underwent a kind of mating fever after finding their matches.

It still surprised her that they'd all found their mates at the same time, but she was starting to suspect that the Pyrosian and Romaki Gods had a wicked sense of timing, and they seemed more than willing to work together.

Vykor seemed to sense her thoughts, lowering his head to brush a kiss to her lips. "It's time, *razdi*."

As if on cue, Hanna blushed and Megan nodded.

"We should—" Hanna said.

"I need to go with Vykor," Lily murmured, embarrassed by the need she heard in her voice.

Megan nodded in agreement. "Karos and I should go, too."

"But we're coming back, right?" Lily wanted to be alone with Vykor, but not forever. She had no idea what all these changes meant, but she wouldn't leave her friends. They were too important to her.

"Of course," Hanna said, but Lily caught an

undertone of uncertainty. Hanna didn't know what would happen, either.

Lily blew out a breath and snuggled deeper into Vykor's arms. She'd worry about that later. Right now, they all needed time alone.

It only took a few minutes to get things organized. Keth and Eva, the couple who ran the Embassy, promised to take care of Cupcake. They were all given communicators, and Megan retrieved the charm from Cupcake's collar and put it back on Lily's bracelet. "I'm not losing you again."

"Not ever," she agreed.

Karos and Vykor were joking with each other, but when Karos threatened to tie his tail in a knot, Vykor snapped a warning that made everyone glance up in alarm. He sucked in a deep breath and apologized. "Sorry, it's hard to think straight right now."

She knew how he felt, but the outburst of anger still surprised her. He'd told her Karos was a friend. Was this what he'd be like now that his dragon had manifested?

The two dragons discussed magical training, and Karos promised to teach Vykor what he could on the flight, with more training once they got back – for all the new dragons. It took her a moment to remember that she was one of them.

Then she caught on to the rest of the conversation and quailed. "We're flying?" She didn't have any of her travel pills with her. Throwing up on her new mate didn't seem like a great way to start what was basically their honeymoon.

Megan winked and laughed. "Don't worry. I'm pretty sure dragons don't get airsick."

She really hoped her friend was right.

She watched in awe as Karos, Megan, and finally Vykor all shifted to their dragon forms. They were beautiful. Karos and Megan were both as big as a city bus and covered with deep crimson scales. They stood side by side, almost identical save for the fact Megan was smaller than her mate and her hide was free of scars.

Vykor stood nearby. In her mind, he was bigger than Karos, though she might be a little biased. She also thought he was the most awe-inspiring of the three. His scales were the deep purple and blue of storm clouds, his talons were all as big as her forearm, and his teeth looked like they could tear through a tank. Her boyfriend was seriously badass.

Vykor lowered his head until his muzzle was right in front of her, and she reached out a hand to stroke him. "You're gorgeous in this form. I know you can't talk right now, but when you can, you're going to have to explain to me why you're purple."

Jet laughed. "He doesn't know either. It was a surprise to us all."

"You'll have to tell me what colour you turn out to be. Stay in touch!" Hanna called.

She started to answer, but all that came out was a squawk of surprise as a mass of blankets appeared from thin air, swaddling her in fluffy warmth. Before she could react, she went soaring into the air and landed firmly on Vykor's back, settled between two of the ridges that rose along his spine.

"Next time, warn me!" She gave the side of his neck a playful slap. "And thank you for the extra blankets."

The massive beast rumbled in acknowledgement, sending a low thrum of vibration through her and triggering another tumult of indecent thoughts. She snuggled deeper into her blankets and hoped no one noticed her flaming cheeks. The *rux* didn't care what form Vykor was in, he was still her mate, and if she didn't have him soon, she was going to lose her mind.

That was the main reason they needed to go so soon after being reunited. The others had consummated their matings, but she and Vykor hadn't. Karos had suggested their courtship had happened slower because Vykor's dragon hadn't been awake at first. It had given them a few precious hours to get to know each other, but their time was up.

She looked across the rain-dampened ground to where Hanna stood with Jet. She couldn't imagine how the two of them had managed it. From what'd heard, they hadn't even been in the same cell.

"I'm learning far too much about my boss' sex life this trip," she muttered to herself, then settled herself more firmly onto Vykor's back and patted his neck. "Ready when you are."

He spread his wings and leapt into the morning air with a bugling cry that echoed off buildings and sent every seagull in the area bolting for cover. It wasn't until they were airborne that it occurred to her this was his first flight. She closed her eyes, gripped the neck ridge in front of her, and called out "I hope you know what you're doing. I heard what happened to Megan on her first landing!"

All three dragons rumbled in amusement, filling the sky around her with a sound like distant thunder.

Sure, it was funny to them. They had wings.

CHAPTER EIGHT

Vykor was surprised to discover that flying was harder than using magic. Magic was more instinctive for him, probably because of all the time he'd spent practicing as a child, desperately hoping his dragon would manifest despite what the priests believed.

Flying, though? There was no way to prepare his mind or his body for that. Not that his body was really his own at the moment. His dragon form was entirely new to him, and while he could have allowed the dragon to take control for this flight, Karos had warned him that wasn't a good idea. If he let the beast become too dominant, they'd struggle to find a balance later. Especially now, while he was in the thrall of the *rux*, his dragon, which represented the more primal side of his nature, would be more difficult to control.

He was angry, too. Enraged at the idea that he'd been lied to all these years. He wanted to scream at the priests and at the Gods themselves for what he'd gone through. The only reason he didn't give in to his fury was the female who sat on his back. Lily was the touchstone that kept him sane and focused. He wouldn't risk hurting or scaring her. She might be a Romaki now, but while dragons were hard to harm and even harder to kill, they could still feel pain. He would never do that to her. She was the only good thing the Gods had ever allowed him, and he intended to love and cherish her every day for the rest of his life.

Karos spoke to him telepathically while they flew, instructing him on flight, magic, and how to control the beast that was now part of him. They talked about what his appearance meant, too, and the fact that Vykor had the magic of both the Snow and Fire clans.

"I don't understand why the Gods did this to me." The telepathic link between Romaki in their dragon form was another element of Romaki life that he'd been denied, but he was grateful to have it now, as well as Karos' counsel.

"I'm no priest, but I think it's a sign of approval of all we've done. Prince Radek found his mate here, and now we have, too. More so, you've become something our species has never seen. This will change everything, Vykor."

"So, you're suggesting that first the Gods made me suffer, and now they're making up for it?" Vykor huffed and a spurt of flame erupted from his mouth.

"I did mention I'm not a priest, didn't I?" Karos said calmly. *"I don't know what the Gods were doing. I do know*

you're angry, but now is not the time for it. You're breathing fire just thinking about this. Let it go and focus on your mate, instead."

He went through the breathing technique he'd been taught as a child, and his anger cooled. His dragon wasn't happy about it, but after a moment's struggle, the beast stopped resisting.

"Free now. Free always," the dragon muttered within his mind.

"Always." He had no intention of locking his dragon away ever again. Why would he?

It was difficult to focus on Karos' instructions and advice, but he managed. Even after they parted ways, Karos kept in contact until they finally flew out of range of the mind link.

Vykor continued flying until he found the perfect location - a snow-covered valley deep in the coastal mountains. There was a small, frozen lake and a stretch of open ground surrounded by a thick forest of evergreens, their branches laden with snow.

"It's beautiful!" Lily called as he banked and started a slow, careful descent.

He had to agree with her. The land out here was breathtaking. He'd seen the mountains from a distance, their deep blue peaks capped with snow, but from his new vantage point they were even more amazing. Vast forests rolled across the foothills like a carpet that shifted slowly from deep green to crisp white as they rose above the treeline. The sea was a barely visible line of green and grey at the horizon, vanishing completely as he spiralled toward the ground.

Lily stayed silent as he lined up his approach, but he could feel her tension, the way her legs clamped tight against his body. He didn't want to screw this up, so he went against Karos' advice and allowed his dragon to take control. It was the right decision. They landed with minimal problems, and Lily uttered a victory cry once they were safely on the ground.

He wasted no time celebrating. He still had a bower to create, and a mate to claim.

LILY WAS STILL TAKING in the beauty of the spot Vykor had chosen for their temporary home when her mate shifted forms. It was difficult for her to wrap her head around the fact that he was both the man and the dragon, but the *rux* wouldn't let her dwell on the point for long. Instead, her attention was caught by the fact he hadn't bothered conjuring clothing. He simply stood in the thigh-deep snow and started chanting softly, his hands weaving patterns in the air.

It was her first chance to see him naked, and he looked even better than she'd imagined. He was fit, lean, and Hollywood levels of handsome. Broad shoulders that tapered to a trim waist, strong arms, powerful thighs, and an ass that should probably be declared a national treasure. Not to mention his erection...hard and thick and rising to the sky, just begging for her attention.

Lust overrode her mind and she walked through the heavy snow to reach him. There were only a few feet between them, but it was too far. She needed to touch him. To taste his mouth and... Whoa. She stopped herself a scant inch before she made contact with him. He needed to focus on what he was doing. Who knew what might happen if she distracted him at the wrong moment during the spell? Magic was something she didn't understand. Not yet, anyway.

She tore her gaze away from her soon-to-be lover and watched what he was creating, instead.

He was facing the lake, drawing up both ice and snow from their surroundings to form a swirling mass that expanded until it was the size of a house. Which, she reminded herself with amusement, was exactly what he was making.

The structure started to form. The shape familiar even if the materials were like nothing she'd ever seen. The walls came first. Shimmering blue-white blocks shot through with shifting threads of red and gold, like flames captured inside ice.

The roof came next, an A-frame design steep enough to shed any snow that might fall, those same impossible frozen flames dancing across the surface.

A door appeared in the front, a single block of ice with a dragon decorating it, the image raised from the surface and tinted the same stormy purple as Vykor's scales.

She didn't speak until Vykor lowered his arms and turned back to take her hand. "This is ours?" she asked.

"This is for you, *sadina*. A symbol of my devotion to you, proof of my intent to love, protect, and cherish you for the rest of our lives." He squeezed her hand and his voice grew thick with emotion. "I never thought I'd be able to do this. Even if I found a mate, I had no magic… not until I found you."

He smiled down at her, his expression a mix of wonder and adoration that took her breath away. "You brought magic into my life, Lily Ashton. You are a gift without price."

"I feel the same way about you, my *sodono*. This time yesterday, my life was utterly ordinary. Today, I've been rescued from imprisonment, healed from my wounds, seen real magic being cast…" She smiled up at him, setting aside all her worries for now. "And fallen head over heels with a dragon."

He uttered a toe-curlingly sexy growl, swept her into his arms, and carried her through the snow to the cabin, and for the first time in her life, she didn't worry about what would come next. There would be no fear, no flinching, no embarrassment over her scars. She didn't know what their future would look like, but she did know this: her fate, and her future, lay with him.

She didn't get to see much as Vykor carried her inside their bower. The air was warm, what furnishings she saw were draped in thick fabrics much like the clothing she wore, and the entire space was lit by the flames trapped within the walls. There was a table set for two, a rock grotto filled with steaming water that somehow didn't melt the ice wall behind it, and a bed so large it would have taken up half of her apartment back in Toronto.

He strode partway to the bed, then stopped, pivoted, and made straight for the bathing grotto instead. "You said you wanted a long, hot shower. How about a bath, instead?"

"That depends. Are you joining me?"

"I'm not leaving your side, *razdi*. Now, or ever again." The rough tone of his voice sent a thrill down her spine, and heat pooled deep in her womb.

"Then a bath sounds wonderful."

His next kiss was different. There was an urgency to it, a hunger that mirrored her own. Their need was raw, rough, and carnal, and she gave herself over to it without hesitation. He kissed her hard on the mouth and then raised her higher to blaze a path down her throat to the rise of her breasts. He sucked one sensitive nipple into his mouth, using his tongue to flick the hardened nub and send sparks racing through her body, flooding every cell and fibre with need.

He stepped over the edge of the bath without raising his head, and sank into the steaming water with a low groan of pleasure.

She knew exactly how he felt. The pleasure of the water was indescribable, the heat chasing the chill from her bones.

Once he was settled, he drew her into his lap, turning her so she faced him, her legs straddling his. He cupped one of her breasts in his palm, using his thumb to toy with her nipple until she was breathless, her head thrown back, eyes closed as she gave herself over to the pleasure of it all.

The *rux* made it easy to let go, to forget the trials and hardships of the day. None of her usual worries affected her, either. She didn't worry about her scars, didn't flinch when he touched her, didn't freeze when the thick head of his cock pressed against the seam of her pussy. She was too far gone to care about anything but him, and it was the most freeing thing in the world.

She moaned and writhed in delight as his mouth dropped to her breast again. This time, he let one of his fangs graze the tender flesh and it sent a zing of pure pleasure straight to her already throbbing clit. She buried her hands in his hair and pulled him closer, grinding their bodies together as the hot water washed over them like a sensual caress.

When it was almost too much to bear, she reached between them and wrapped her hand around the hard length of his cock. Hard ridges lined the shaft, which was so thick her fingers could barely span it. She moved her hand up and down his length with slow, deliberate movements, measuring him inch by inch, learning the feel of him as he continued to feast on her breasts.

His groans filled the air as he thrust his cock into her hand. Every rock of his hips sent water sloshing against the rocky edge of the pool. He played with her breasts, using his fingers and tongue to bring her to the verge of orgasm without letting her cross over.

"Vykor. I...I need--" she stammered, unsure how to ask for what she wanted.

He lifted his head and gave her a wicked smile that made her heart pound even faster. "More?"

"Yes. God, yes."

"Leave the Gods out of this," he muttered before sealing her mouth with his in a kiss so hot she thought the water around them might start to boil.

He lifted her again, setting her on a level shelf of rock she swore hadn't existed a moment ago. She was almost completely out of the water, now, and he moved between her legs, parting them with gentle but insistent pressure.

"Let me give you what you need."

She nodded, suddenly aware of how exposed she was, and for a moment her doubts came back. What did he see when he looked at her? Had he noticed the scars that marked her body, silent reminders of a childhood full of darkness and violence?

She moved a hand, covering one of the scars on her stomach, but he moved it away gently. Then, he raked his gaze over her, touching the circular scar left by one of her father's cigarettes, the one she'd tried to hide. "Your scars are a testament to your strength, *sadina*. They are part of you. And you are beautiful."

Her doubts vanished, seared away by the heat in his voice and the fires that burned in his eyes. He moved into the space between her thighs and lowered his head to press an open-mouthed kiss to the soft flesh of her inner thigh. His beard was rough against her skin, an erotic contrast to the gentle touch of his mouth.

She moaned, and he moved again, this time to lift her legs and drape them over his shoulders. She leaned back against the rocks that cradled her at the perfect angle to watch as he leaned in and buried his head between her thighs. He went straight for her clit, sucking the delicate pearl into his mouth and lashing it with his tongue. Stars exploded in her vision, and just when she felt like she couldn't take anymore, he slid two fingers into her channel, curving them so his fingertips hit a sensitive spot she didn't even know she had.

"Vykor!" His name rose from her lips in a shocked gasp, and then she was falling, tumbling into a breathless bliss as her orgasm bloomed.

THE *RUX HAD* him ensnared and he wasn't even trying to resist any longer. All he wanted was Lily. Her scent was a drug, her taste as intoxicating as the finest liquor. He rose out of the water and took her in his arms again, drawing her back into the pool.

She wrapped her arms and legs around him, slick skin sliding over his as they sank back into the water, mouths already fused together in a kiss that was already better than any sex he'd ever had.

"Need you," he told her when he next broke the kiss to breathe.

"Yes. Need you, too."

That was all he needed to hear. He moved back to one of the ledges he'd crafted into the stone and drew her into his lap, arranging her limbs so she was straddling him again. He kissed her hard as he guided their bodies together, barely biting back a groan of raw pleasure when he finally slid home.

She moaned, the sound vibrating against his lips and tongue. It was a low, needy sound that broke the last threads of his control. She was so tight around him that every flex of her inner walls was almost painfully intense, and he knew it would only get better.

He rolled his hips, arching upward to drive himself deeper, and she moaned again, her hands on his shoulders as she braced herself against his thrusts.

She kept her eyes open, and he found himself lost in their violet depths. This was his mate, his *sadina*. Now, and forever. That knowledge drove him to new heights of passion, and he powered into her, his hands gripping her hips, controlling the pace, and at the same time, keeping her balanced above him.

They raced each other to the heights of pleasure, too caught up in each other to take things slow. There'd be time for that, later. He wanted to unwrap her like a present, discovering her secrets one by one, but for now, all he wanted was her.

The rhythm of their lovemaking grew wild and erratic, and as he hurtled toward orgasm he reached between them, pressing the pad of his finger to her clit. He wanted to bring her over with him. Her inner walls gripped him hard, pulsating around his cock as she came. His fangs ached with a sudden urge to bite her, but he didn't give in. The next time he did that, they'd do it together, cementing their bond.

Just the thought of her biting him took him over the edge and he exploded into release, crying out her name as he emptied himself inside her.

Once the storm of their passion began to ebb, he folded her into his arms and held tight, their bodies still connected. For the first time in his life, he felt whole. He had his mate and his dragon, their presences filling him with a sense of peace and belonging he'd never imagined possible.

Lily stirred in his arms, looking around the bower he'd created for her. "I still can't believe you made all this for me. It's…" she raised a dripping hand to gesture around them. "I don't have the words to describe how amazing this is. Especially since you've only had your magic for a short time."

"Karos had a few suggestions," he admitted. The older dragon had been generous with his ideas, support, and wisdom. He owed the male a debt of thanks he'd be more than happy to repay once they were together again.

"But you made it happen. I don't know the rituals of your species, Vykor, but I imagine there's a moment when I'm supposed to accept this gift and what it means." Soft fingers, still wet from the pool, touched his cheek. "This place pleases me. Hell, it amazes me! And so do you, my mate. Very much."

A fierce sense of pride tore through him. "And you please me, *sadina*. So much my heart is full." He basked in the moment, knowing that he would spend the rest of his life trying to make her as happy as they were now.

CHAPTER NINE

VYKOR SLIPPED OUT of bed without waking Lily. The *rux* had taxed them both to the limits of their endurance, driving them into each other's arms again and again. They'd lost themselves in the all-consuming madness of the mating fever, making up for the time they'd lost. Waiting had been necessary, but now that he knew what he'd been resisting, it was hard not to have regrets. If he'd claimed her right away, she would never have been hurt. Assuming the claiming would have worked, that is. Until his dragon had manifested, it might not have.

He looked back at his mate, her naked body only partially covered by a blanket and felt a sudden need to return to bed. He could wrap himself around her, protect her while she slept. But he didn't. He was thinking clearly for the first time in days, and there were questions he needed answered. Answers only his dragon could provide.

He walked to the bathing grotto he'd made for them, pausing on the way to pick up the communicator they'd brought with them. Once he was settled in the steaming water, he worked his way through the messages, reading some, archiving others for later, and listening to the voice messages left by his friends and their mates. They'd spoken a few times since parting company, ensuring everyone was still safe.

Jet and Hanna were back at the embassy, and their updates included news about who had been charged, how the humans were reacting to the news, and how the search for other malcontents was going. So far, Kyle appeared to have been the only one, but the investigation was far from over. They wouldn't stop until they were sure the embassy was secure.

It turned out that Kyle's recruitment hadn't been a question of belief in the cause, it had been about money. By the time he realized they had no intention of paying him what they'd promised, his part was already done, and he'd been left with no choice but to stay with the group in hopes they'd protect him. He'd been more than happy to discuss everything he knew with the authorities. Unfortunately, it hadn't been much.

The last message was marked as being from the Temple of Solun, on Romak. He set the unit aside without playing the message. He wasn't ready to deal with them. Not until he had some answers.

"Why have you only manifested now?" he sent the thought to his dragon.

"Prisoner. Walls. Constrained me." It was the same

answer as before, but he didn't understand it any better the second time.

"*What walls? Who imprisoned you?*" he pressed.

"*You.*"

A tendril of pure ice coiled around his heart and he shivered despite being surrounded by hot water. "*No! It wasn't me. I spent my life waiting and hoping you'd appear.*"

"*Your walls,*" the dragon insisted.

"*Explain.*"

"*Too much control. All the time. Could not move. You would not hear me. I slept. Waited. Then you found her. She called. Made me strong. I am free now.*"

The dragon's simple explanation filled him first with horror, then fury. "*Too much control? You couldn't manifest because of the priests' insistence that I control my anger? That's why I was without you all these years?*"

"*Yes.*"

Frost and Flame, he'd done it to himself. Convinced the priests were right and he was born without a dragon's spirit, he'd locked himself down, channelled his anger and resentment into his research, never letting it out. Never even admitting it was there. Gods! He wanted to scream in fury and frustration. Lily had seen the truth right away. He hadn't been rejected by the Gods, he'd belonged to both of them. But the only ones who should have known it, who were supposed to speak for the Lord of Frost and the Lady of Flame, had been so convinced of their own theories they hadn't heard their Gods.

He'd struggled to find a place for himself, to accept

what he was. Now he was something else. He held out a hand, summoning a swirling orb of violet energy a few inches above his palm, then dismissing it with a flick of his fingers.

He was a dragon, but he was still a misfit. He had magic, but it wasn't like any other Romaki's. *Who am I? What am I?* He'd sought the answers to those questions once, and now, he needed to answer those same questions again. All because he'd listened to the priests and locked away a part of himself because he thought it was the right thing to do.

"I was such a fool." He rose from the water, conjuring a robe the moment his feet hit the floor. He wanted to wake Lily and tell her what he'd learned, but she was exhausted. He'd let her rest a little longer. Besides, there was one more thing he needed to do, first.

He picked up the communicator and carried it outside with him, moving far enough from the structure there was no chance Lily would be woken by the incoming message. The forest was quiet, even the occasional creak of branches muffled by the snow. It was almost midday, but the sun was hidden behind heavy cloud cover, dark with the threat of snow.

The message was a pre-recorded hologram, so he took a moment to reshape a section of snow into a table and placed the unit on top of it. Then, he activated the message and stepped back to watch.

He didn't recognize the pair of Romaki shown in the projection, though their attire was familiar enough. The male was a priest of Solun, the female was from the Order of Daga, and both of them wore an elaborate seal on a chain around their necks. These weren't simple priests, they were the High Priests of the Temples, and they wanted to talk to him.

He bared his fangs and snarled, already aware that whatever they had to say, he wasn't going to like it. Not now he knew the truth. He might have been the one to lock away part of himself, but he'd done it at the instruction of priests like these.

The female spoke first. "Greetings Vykor Halek. Word of your transformation has reached us, and we wished to send our congratulations. Welcome to the skies." She intoned the ritualistic words.

"Indeed. Welcome to the skies, and congratulations on the claiming of your human mate." The male priest's expression turned sour for a moment. "Though by now, I assume you have claimed her, and thus she is no longer human, but a proper Romaki."

He already didn't like where this was going. A proper Romaki? What in the name of Solun's frosty balls did that even mean?

The male continued speaking. "I trust you already understand the importance of your transformation, not only for yourself, but for all Romaki. Once we have verified that you wield the powers of both Solun and Daga, it will be a powerful sign that the Gods wish us to continue exploring the cosmos and expanding our influence over other worlds and cultures."

The female shot a look of irritation at her

companion. "Expansion can wait. You represent hope and healing for our species, a symbol for all to look upon as we seek to heal after the unrest and horrors of war."

The priest shrugged. "Perhaps. What we can agree on, is that you need to come home, Son of Romak. For the good of all your species, you are needed here. You and your mate will return as soon as possible so that we may verify your abilities and then train you to use them. If the reports are true, then you have tremendous powers, and you will need to learn how to wield them properly. A ship is already being arranged to carry you and your mate home," the male said.

"Once your time of seclusion is over, of course," the female added.

Anger tore through him, leaving his soul raw. Now, they wanted him back? Not because they cared about him, but because of what he represented. "Not happening."

He had heard enough. He paused the recording, leaving the hologram of the two priests suspended in the air over the snow-crafted table. A Son of Romak? He'd been treated as an outcast for his entire life. An ancient law prevented him from even knowing his name or lineage. The priest had named him, and they hadn't used a lot of imagination doing it. Vykor Halek literally translated to the lost one from Halek, the town where he'd been found. If they hadn't given up on him, he might have come into his powers years ago. What right did they have to command him to come back now?

His anger grew as he replayed the message in his mind. He had no interest in helping the temples spread their influence, and even less in becoming a religious symbol. If they wanted to verify his powers, they could come to Earth. He'd be happy to give them a personal demonstration! He paced in circles around the table, growing angrier with every circuit.

"Learn to wield my powers properly? You don't even know what they are! You denied I could have them in the first place." He stormed away from the table, letting his fury overtake him as an act of defiance to the ones who had taught him to control it in the first place. They'd beaten him down and used him as an example of the Gods' displeasure. Now, they wanted to use him again. It would never happen. "My *sadina* will never be a proper Romaki, and neither will I!"

The change took him unawares and in a matter of heartbeats he had taken to the skies as a dragon. As he flew, he gave voice to his fury, his bellows loud enough to shake the snow from the trees beneath him.

His anger burned hotter than the heart of a star as he let himself revisit every bitter memory of his childhood. He would have done anything to escape, but he couldn't. The priests had banned all travel off-planet, claiming it was the Gods' will. The priests. It all came back to them. They'd done this, and he'd allowed it because he hadn't known any better.

It took longer than he should have to realize that

not all the anger he felt was his own, and longer still for him to let go of his fury and start to think rationally again. They'd been right about one thing: he didn't know how to be a dragon. He'd spent his entire adult life being something else. Lily didn't know how to be a dragon, either. As her mate, he should be the one to teach her, but how could he, when he barely knew what he was doing? Doubts tore at him, as sharp and cold as the mountain winds that screamed past his wings.

He was far from the valley when it finally dawned on him. He had never made the decision to shift forms. He hadn't even considered it, but here he was. His dragon had done it on his own. *So much for being in control.* Even his dragon had more say in his actions than he did. That would have to change.

"We need to go back," he told the beast as he tried to wrest control away.

"Never going back. Free!"

"To Romak? Never. To Lily. We need to go back to Lily."

The beast didn't answer, but some of the anger swirling inside him started to fade, and he regained partial control. It was enough for him to slow their flight and begin a long, sweeping turn that would take him back to their valley, and their mate.

"Lily. Protect. Ours."

"Which we aren't doing right now, because you flew away...and I let it happen." Karos had been right. Keeping the balance between the two parts of his nature wasn't easy, and he'd screwed it up. Badly.

"Go back. Protect," the beast sounded chagrined, and a second later it receded to the back of his mind.

He tightened the turn and winged his way back toward their valley. Romaki youth all underwent a period of adjustment while learning to live with the dual parts of their nature. Both he and his dragon had scars created over the years they'd been kept apart. It was going to take time to work through them all. He could see that, now.

"I will never lock you away again. And we are never going to allow anyone else to control us. We are free, now."

There was no answer save for a rumble of approval from the beast. For now, that would be enough. Later, when the *rux* was over and he could think clearly, the two of them would have to find their balance. At least they had one thing they could always agree on. Lily.

He shouldn't have left her alone, though the valley was safe enough. The nearest humans would be dozens of kilometres away at least, and the local carnivores would all be hibernating through the heaviest part of the winter. Still, he wouldn't let himself lose control like that again. She was too precious to risk.

LILY DIDN'T KNOW what had woken her, but something felt wrong. Had she heard a dragon's roar, or was that just something from her dreams? She'd been dreaming of dragons for days, now. No surprise there. All her good dreams had been about Vykor, dragons, and magic. Her nightmares, and there had been a few, had featured John hurting her, mocking her from somewhere out of sight. In those dreams she'd been powerless, her limbs like lead, her mind screaming in fear as the moment she'd been shot playing out again and again.

In the short periods of time the *rux* allowed them between bouts of lovemaking, she and Vykor had spoken in-depth about her new abilities. He'd introduced her to the basic idea of magic and conveyed the advice Karos had given him on their flight into the mountains.

On top of all that, her dragon had started speaking to her. It was a lot to process, and she was still trying to make sense of it all.

"Wake." Her dragon gave her a mental nudge, and she belatedly realized that was what had woken her a moment before.

"Why?" she asked aloud.

"Mate gone."

"What? When?"

"Not long. Flew away."

Unease fluttered in her belly and she hopped out of bed, bare feet slapping against the warm floor. Even after two days, she was still fascinated by the magic that surrounded them. The entire building, including the furnishings, was made of what she swore was ice, but it didn't melt, even after Vykor had done something to the floor when she complained about cold feet. She still couldn't manage the simplest of spells, and her dragon hadn't done more than speak a few words. It was frustrating. Vykor had managed to transform, kick ass, and build them an entire bower less than a day after his dragon appeared. But here she was, still a basic, boring, human.

The place felt empty without Vykor's presence, and her unease ratcheted up another notch. She couldn't protect herself, yet. Vykor knew that. So, where was he, and why had he left her?

The events of the last few days had reopened wounds she thought long healed. She startled easily and found herself falling into old habits. She kept her head down when she talked, spoke softer than normal, and was always aware of the nearest exit in case she needed to escape. She hated feeling this way. She'd worked for years to overcome those behaviours.

"You are a freaking dragon, remember? At least, you will be eventually. You're going to be a fire-breathing, bad-guy busting badass. Megan said I'm bulletproof now. Bulletproof! So, no more flinching. No more hiding. You don't need Vykor around to feel safe. You don't need anyone for that."

The pep talked helped a little, but she still felt uneasy. Probably because she couldn't do any of the things a real Romaki could. Maybe if she tried again...

She stood still, closed her eyes, and spoke the incantation Vykor had taught her, visualizing herself in similar garments to the ones he'd created for her the day of their escape. Nothing happened. She was still naked.

"Some dragon I am." She donned one of the outfits Vykor had conjured for her. She chose a white tunic, leggings, and boots this time, whimsically matching them to the snow outside.

A quick search of their temporary home turned up no clues to where Vykor had gone, or why. There was no note, and nothing was out of place. The only thing that struck her as odd was the fact their communicator was missing. They'd taken to leaving it on the table, but it wasn't there, now.

"If he left me here with no way to call for help and no idea how to fly back home, I'll tie him to the bed by his tail!" She poured herself some hot *korta*, taking a moment to breathe in the fruit-scented steam. She'd taken a liking to the deliciousness that was the Romaki's version of coffee. It was perfect, like everything else Vykor had created. The food, the furniture, even their bower had all come from him. While she couldn't manage to conjure up so much as a spark.

"*Soon*," her dragon said, the tone almost childlike in its glee.

"*You said that yesterday*," She retorted sourly. She wanted to make the flight back under her own power, and they'd be leaving by the end of the day.

"If I were a dragon with a communicator and some reason to use it, where would I go?" she mused to herself as she wandered around their bower, sipping her drink.

"Oh, I know! I'd go outside, so as not to disturb my

sleeping mate." That seemed like something Vykor would do. She couldn't see him leaving her with no means of communication.

She left their little house and stepped out into a winter wonderland. Snowflakes as big as goose feathers fell out of the slate grey sky, the clouds filtering the sunlight so that it looked closer to twilight than midday. Marshmallow mounds of snow covered everything in sight, softening the world around her. Her breath frosted the air as she followed Vykor's tracks in the snow to a table that hadn't been there the last time she'd been outside. A holographic projection hovered a few inches above the surface showing a male and a female dressed in ornate robes. The figures danced and shimmered as snowflakes passed through them.

He'd paused the message and walked away. She could see his tracks heading toward the lake, a massive indentation in the snow where he'd shifted to his dragon form, and then nothing at all.

She turned back to the projection. If she played it back, maybe she could find out what had upset him.

That's when she heard the crunch of boots on snow and realized she wasn't alone.

"Men come," her dragon informed her.

"You're sure?"

"Listen. Smell. Your senses are mine."

Right. She still wasn't used to using her new senses and her brain tended to filter out the extra input to avoid overloading. She made a conscious effort to really sense what was around her, and new information flooded into her. The scent of evergreens, the whispered hiss of snowflakes blowing across the frozen ground. She could smell Vykor, too, traces of his scent still hung in the air near where she stood.

Then she heard it again, clearer this time. Booted feet stomping through snow. She turned toward the sound and inhaled. Three men. She could smell their sweat and hear the noise of their passage as they trudged through the deep snow. Another scent struck her, one she remembered from the aftermath of their rescue. It was acrid and unmistakable. Guns. She wasn't sure how she knew, but she did. There were three men coming this way, and at least one of them was armed. Shit. Shit. Shit.

Her dragon huffed. *"We are strong. They are not."*

"But I can't do any magic, yet. I'm not ready for advanced dragon to asshole combat. Especially if I can't even turn into a dragon!" Wait. Maybe they weren't here for her at all. Maybe they were just hunters. She dismissed the thought as soon as it appeared. This was national parkland. No hunting allowed. At best, the men were poachers and at worst... shit.

"Now would be a really good time for you to make an appearance," she muttered out loud.

Her dragon snorted with amusement. Apparently, she wasn't overly concerned about the trouble headed their way. *"If trouble comes, we face it together."*

The footsteps were getting closer, and she was still standing out in the open. Step one, get out of sight. She darted behind the cabin and into the woods. If she went back inside, she'd be a sitting duck....er... dragon.

Once she was hunkered down behind some bushes, she tried extending her senses again. It was easier this time. Probably because she was scared. *Yay, adrenaline.*

The men were definitely headed this way, and they were talking to each other as they moved.

"You sure that tracking dingus is working right?"

"It's working. Just another hundred meters or so."

"Wouldn't we see tracks or something by now if they were up here?"

"She's with a dragon, you idiot. He flew her up here. No tracks if you're in the fucking air," a third male chimed in.

"Jeez, Trent. I'm just asking. No need to be an asshole about it."

"I'm not paid to be nice. Deal with it."

The first man barked out a laugh. "None of us are getting paid for this. No one left to pay us."

The one they called Trent spoke again. "True. But orders are orders. Ashton wanted things taken care of, and we're going to follow through. He might be gone, but the battle continues, right?"

Two other voices muttered in agreement, but they didn't sound overly enthusiastic.

"John told us that if anything happened to him, see to it the blonde got the same treatment. Fair is fair, right? Now, as it happens, that same blonde has taken up with one of those dragons. We can't hurt him directly, but we can hurt her. She's only human, right?

So, we take her out, Ashton's avenged, and we send a message to the women of Earth - be loyal to your species or face the consequences," Trent drawled.

Charming. No wonder these idiots can't get dates. Given a choice between them and any of the aliens she'd met, she'd take the alien option every time.

"*No other options. Only mate,*" her dragon scolded her.

"*Only Vykor,*" she agreed. "*But I'm still going to yell at him for leaving me alone to deal with the trouble headed our way.*"

"*No trouble. Flame. Fwoosh. Gone.*" Her dragon sounded alarmingly happy at the idea.

"*There are three of them and one of me. Also, I don't know how to do the flame fwoosh thing yet.*" She caught herself gesturing as if she were having a normal conversation and stuffed her hands into her sleeves. Bad enough she was talking to a voice in her head. No sense adding to the level of crazy, even if no one was around to see her.

"*We have advantage.*"

"*How's that?*" she asked, already certain she wasn't going to like the answer.

"*They think you are alone.*"

"*I am alone.*" And boy, was Vykor going to hear about that when he got back.

"*Not alone. We are one.*"

Before she could reply, she heard something behind her and spun toward the noise. Son of a bitch, there were four men out there, not three.

The fourth man was holding a rifle in his hands, the

barrel pointed straight at her chest. "Stand up and turn around. I'll make this quick."

She rose, surprised to note that her legs were steady and her hands weren't shaking. Her fear was gone, replaced by a growing sense of fury. She'd been beaten down too many times. Threatened by too many jerks like this one. She was done being bullied. "I won't."

The man cocked his head. "What's that?"

She fisted her hands at her sides, squared her shoulders, and spoke in a voice she barely recognized. "I'm not going to make this quick, or painless. You don't deserve it."

He raised the gun to his shoulder.

She raised her fists to the sky and summoned her dragon, hoping like hell this time it worked. "Now!"

She braced herself for pain that never came. Instead, she simply ceased to be one thing and became something else. Something much, much bigger.

Her dragon roared in exaltation, and then all hell broke loose.

—————

CHAPTER TEN

—————

Vykor was still out of sight of the valley when a sound tore through his mind. One so powerful it made him flap and flail in the air in shock. It was the battle cry of another dragon. But that didn't make any sense. There weren't any other dragons around. Karos was out of range with his mate...Mate. Dragon. *Lily!*

"We go!" His stunned senses were sent reeling with the force of his dragon's declaration. *Did none of the beasts have volume control?*

He didn't bother agreeing with his dragon. He just flew as hard and fast as he could for the valley where he'd left his mate sleeping.

"Lily! What's happened?" he hurled the thought towards his mate's mind.

"Trouble happened. Get back here fast or you'll miss it."

"Miss what? How are you a dragon? Are you alright?"

"Humanity Firsters are here. Four of them. I shifted when someone tried to shoot me."

"Protect!" his dragon interjected, skimming over the treetops at breakneck speed.

"Are you injured?" It wasn't likely —his species were notoriously hard to kill, but it was possible… and he'd left her alone. Frost and Flames. He'd left his mate alone.

"I might need a little help reining in my uh…more destructive half. The lightning is making a mess of the forest."

"Lightning? We can't throw lightning!"

"Wanna bet?" Lily sounded almost gleeful.

What in the name of the Lady of Flames was happening? He crested the ridge of their valley and finally got a look at what was going on. A bolt of golden lightning streaked across the valley, leaving a path of scorched foliage and melted snow in its wake. Trees popped, the sound like the cheerful crackle of logs on a fireplace, only on a far larger scale.

He followed the path of destruction back to its source. Lily stood in the middle of a scorched clearing, the remains of trees and other foliage smouldering all around her. She was magnificent, her dark purple scales gleaming in the light, her wings extended as she roared and loosed another blast of lightning from her jaws.

He roared in response.

"Did you see? I can throw lightning!"

"I saw. I don't understand, but I saw. Are you alright? Where are the attackers? I'll finish them for you."

Lily furled her wings and snorted, sending twin puffs of smoke into the air. *"I already took care of them."*

"Then why are you still throwing lightning bolts?"

He landed in the clearing next to her, somehow managing to touch down without tripping over the mess of shattered trees and soggy, freshly thawed ground.

"Because it's fun? And honestly, I have no idea how I did any of this. I told you, I need help getting my dragon reined in. She's in charge right now, and she's not listening to me!"

"I know the feeling." He moved in beside her and draped a wing over her back. *"I'm here. I'm sorry I wasn't here before. Your first transformation should have been special."*

"Oh, it was special alright." One of the smoking trees burst into flames. She turned her head and squelched the fire with a blast of ice breath. Gods, how was she doing that?"

"Can you breathe fire, too?"

Amused pride thrummed through their connection. *"Yep. I'm like the Swiss Army knife of dragons. An attack for every purpose and occasion."* She paused a beat, then asked. *"So, what do I look like right now? Apart from big, purple, and scaly. I can see enough of myself to figure out that much."*

"I have never seen another dragon as lovely as you are, my sadina. *You're the same colour I am, like a storm cloud come to life. Deep blues and purples, with a silvery sheen to your scales that makes it look like you are touched with frost."*

She rumbled and leaned into him. *"Keep talking. She likes hearing you talk."*

He twined his neck around hers, careful to stay clear

of her muzzle in case she decided to throw more magic around. *"I'm sorry I left you alone. I got a message from Romak that upset me. I should have talked to you about it, but my dragon took control and decided to fly off in a rage."*

"Seems to be a lot of that going around."

"If I had any idea that you were in danger, I never would have left."

"I know." Her body relaxed into his. *"Can you tell me how to shift back? Talking this way is giving me a headache."*

"Tell your dragon it's time to step back. Then envision yourself in your other form."

She was quiet for a moment, then sighed in frustration. *"She says she likes this form and wants to stay like this for a while."*

"Tell her if she doesn't let you change now, then I won't take her flying later today."

A few seconds later, Lily had shifted back. She looked so tiny beside him. Tiny, perfect, and naked.

She gave him a cheeky grin. "That worked. Are you joining me or are you going to thtand there looking all majethtic for a while longer?"

He shifted forms, turned, and pulled her into his arms. His hands skimmed over her, searching for injuries even while he enjoyed exploring her naked body. He'd never tire of touching her. Every curve, dimple, and scar fascinated him.

"You're naked," she pointed out as he held her.

"You were naked first. I just followed your lead."

"Oopth. I forgot." Her wide smile told him it wasn't

an accident at all. It also revealed a new sign of her transformation. Her fangs had appeared.

"Why am I lithping?"

"Fangs." He told her.

She squealed in delight and raised her fingers to her mouth. "I haf fangth!"

"You do."

"Doth thif mean I get to bwite you?"

The idea sent a tidal wave of lust crashing over him. He wanted to feel her teeth on his skin. Nipping. Teasing, biting…

"*Claiming,*" his dragon chimed in.

"Frost and Flames, yes." She could claim him now, completing the mating ritual he'd started the day he'd converted her. He wanted that more than anything. But first, he needed to apologize…and then he needed to confirm that the men who had come for them were truly dead. He'd taken enough chances with her safety for one lifetime already.

"Fost and fwames…" She scowled. "I thound thilly."

"You sound adorable. You'll get used to them quickly. Megan barely lisped at all when we spoke with her yesterday, remember?"

Lily nodded.

"I need to apologize properly to you. I gave up control to my other half, indulging in my anger instead of facing it. I'm sorry I wasn't here for you when you needed me."

She tipped her head to one side, and when she spoke, she uttered each word carefully to avoid lisping. "I'm not sorry. I think I needed this. I've been afraid for so much of my life. Avoiding conflict. Staying quiet even when I had something I wanted to say. Megan and Hanna have been encouraging me to be braver, and I have been, but today, I stood up to the ones trying to hurt me. I stopped them. By mythelf."

She paused, then laughed and tapped her temple. "I haf been reminded I had a little help."

"Your dragon is part of you. She might have her own voice, but she's still a part of you. You did this." He gestured around the ruined forest. "I didn't even know we could wield lightning. You did all this on your own, on instinct!"

"And made a meth – ugh, a mess – doing it."

"I don't know how to fix this, but I'm sure Karos can. He's had centuries to master his spellcraft. We'll ask him to fly here before returning to the embassy."

Lily winced, looking sheepish. "Yeah. Uh. About that."

"What?"

"One of the lightning bolts kind of zthigged when I wanted it to zthag." She pointed. The snow table he'd crafted was gone, along with the communicator. All that was left was a melted stretch of snow and scorched ground.

"Got a little carried away, did you?"

She slowed her speech again so she could enunciate around her fangs. "It is a lot of fun. Try one. You'll see."

"How?"

She shrugged. "I was trying for fwoosh and got bzzzt zap instead."

"That…is not terribly helpful, *sadina*."

She grinned, flashing her fangs at him. "You're a smart dragon. You'll figure it out."

"Not as smart as my mate." She'd shifted without help. Summoned magic with minimal instruction, and come to terms with her new reality far faster than he had. The Gods had made more than a few mistakes with him, but choosing Lily as his mate made up for at least some of them.

He conjured a heavy cloak and boots for Lily, draping her in his colours and ensuring she stayed warm. She might not feel the cold the way she used to, but standing barefoot in slushy snow still wasn't comfortable.

"Be right back."

He moved away from her, picking his way through the charred splinters of what had once been a stand of evergreens. Once he was a safe distance, he shifted forms again. This time he stayed still for a few minutes, using his senses and higher viewpoint to locate the bodies of the four men who had come after Lily. They were definitely dead. His sweet Lily had killed them. At some point, she'd have to come to terms with what she'd done. They'd both killed in self-defence, but once the *rux* had faded, they'd both feel the full weight of their actions. He'd be there for her, just as he knew she'd be there for him.

It finally hit him. He wasn't alone anymore. Lily would be with him. At his side. Guarding his back, sharing in every moment of laughter and sorrow. He'd flown off today because there'd never been anyone he could turn to before. He had always coped with every challenge alone. That wasn't the case anymore. He had his *razdi* to light his way.

He threw back his head and bellowed to the sky, a clarion cry of pure joy he hoped would carry to the ears of his Gods. It wasn't a thank you. He wasn't ready for that. But it was an acknowledgement.

After that, he visualized the lightning bolt he'd seen as he flew into the valley. When he had it in mind, he turned his head, aimed for an already destroyed part of the forest, and loosed a sizzling bolt of magic that was different than anything he'd felt before. It worked. Elation and wonder filled him. *I can wield lightning.*

He shifted back, not bothering with clothing as he strode towards Lily, who was clapping and cheering. Gods, he loved having her encouragement.

He paused and reflected on that as he lifted her into his arms and headed for their bower, making his way through the partially melted snow. He didn't just love her encouragement. He loved *her*.

"FROST, FIRE, AND FWOOSHES." Vykor muttered as he scooped her into his arms.

"What was that?"

"I've invented a new expression. One only you and I can use, since we're the only ones who can throw lightning bolts."

"The fwoosh was for fire, though."

He grinned. "I still like it. Besides, frost, fire and zap doesn't have the same ring to it."

"Lacks the alliteration angle," she agreed, barely repressing a giggle. She felt wonderful. Not drunk exactly, or intoxicated the way the *rux* made her feel, but she was definitely under the influence of something. Adrenaline, maybe? Accomplishment at standing up for herself? Or maybe it was relief that she'd survived. She didn't really care what it was, as long as it didn't go away any time soon.

He pushed the door open with his hip and carried her straight to the bed. When he set her down on the blankets, she noted he'd added another layer, these ones warmed as if they had come straight out of the dryer. She snuggled deeper into them, letting the warmth sink in. "You'll have to teach me that trick. I love getting into a nice, toasty warm bed on a cold day."

He stretched out beside her, and she barely noticed when he waved his hand and banished her few pieces of clothing back to wherever he'd conjured them from. "I'll teach you all my tricks. There will be no secrets between us, love."

"No thecreth," she agreed, too happy to worry about her pronunciation.

Feeling brazen, she rose to one elbow and kissed

him, then slowly worked her way down his body. She'd memorized so much of him, the way his muscles felt beneath her hands, the taste of his skin, the way he groaned when she found a particularly sensitive spot.

She took her time, deliberately moving from one sensitive spot to another with featherlight touches of her lips, stringing them together in an erotic game of connect the dots. By the time she reached his cock, his body was taut with anticipation. She pressed a kiss to the crown of his cock, then parted her lips and took him inside her mouth with slow, measured movements. She was careful of her new fangs, using them to gently graze his length, easing them over the ridges that ringed his shaft.

He placed a hand on her head, guiding her without forcing her, his fingers tangling in her hair as he started pumping in and out of her mouth. "Gods, that's good. Don't stop."

She didn't speak, only hummed a little and wrapped one hand around the base of his shaft, pumping it in time to his thrusts, and she didn't stop until his hand stilled her head and he uttered a low groan. "Don't want to finish like this. Want to be inside you when you claim me."

She raised her head, releasing him. "Claim you?"

He raised his head to smile down at her. "Bite me. Claim me. Complete the ritual, now that you have fangs of your own."

"I don't want to hurt you."

"You won't." He stroked her hair, staring at her with open hunger. "It won't hurt either of us. I promise."

She trusted him. More than any man she'd ever known. "Okay. Wait. Either of us? Are you going to bite me, too?"

He bared his fangs. "I'd like to. With your permission, of course."

"And it won't hurt?"

"There will be nothing but pleasure in this joining. I would never hurt you."

"Okay." She sat up. "Uh… how?"

"On your hands and knees, my lovely mate. I'll show you."

She moved into position, legs spread, head down, arms braced.

"Perfect," the word came out with enough of a rumble she knew his dragon was present.

Her beast stirred in response. *"Claim. Ours."*

He moved behind her, running his hands down her flanks to her hips. One hand stayed there, the other reached between them to stroke the slick lips of her pussy. She shivered in delight and pressed back against his fingers. He kept up the slow caresses for several minutes, priming her body until she was aching for more than just his touch. She needed his cock inside her, and she needed it now.

"More," she pleaded.

"It would be my pleasure." He placed the thick head of his cock just outside the entrance to her channel, then pushed himself inside her with a slow, steady thrust.

"Yes!" She rocked back, moving far faster than he was.

"Patience, *razdi*."

"Not today," her voice reverberated low in her throat, revealing her dragon's frustration.

"Ah," he withdrew then thrust again, harder this time. "We'll do slow another time, then."

"Another time," she agreed, squeezing her inner walls around him.

"Gods, do that again and I won't last long."

She glanced over her shoulder and grinned at him, flexing her body around him yet again. "That?"

"*Sadina…*" the sound was more growl than an actual word.

She flexed again, swaying her hips from side to side as she did. Vykor's control snapped. She wanted him wild, needed to feel how much he desired her. How much he cared for her.

He leaned over her, pressed a light kiss to her back, then clamped his hands to her hips and took her hard. She had to brace herself as he powered into her, every stroke sending her higher into orbit. Passion filled her, a swirling storm of light and heat that consumed her from the inside out. She sank into the thick blankets atop the bed, fingers kneading the fabric in time to his thrusts.

The flickering lights from the walls played across her field of vision, the sounds of desire rose up around them, and the fruity perfume of *korta* blended with the musky scents of sex.

When she was trembling on the edge of orgasm he leaned over her, his chest touching her back, his ragged breath fanning over the nape of her neck. Instinctively, she tilted her head to one side, baring her throat to him.

"Mine," he said, then sank his fangs into her neck. Her senses spun, then shattered into shards of crystalline bliss. She cried out in mindless pleasure, only to have her cry muffled against Vykor's wrist. Her fangs tingled and she instinctively bit down.

Her dragon roared in triumph, and his blood flowed into her, along with something else. She didn't understand how, but she knew it was Vykor, or part of him. The essence of all he was poured into her, binding them together, heart to heart and soul to soul. She saw all of him, and he saw all of her. It was incredible, intimate, and achingly beautiful. She clung to the moment as long as she could, not wanting to let go of him, afraid that once it was gone, she'd never get this feeling back. He was her soulmate, and she never wanted to be without him again.

"With him, always," her dragon murmured, a contented voice in the back of her mind.

She realized the beast was right. The sensation was fading, but it didn't leave her completely. She could still feel part of Vykor inside her, filling the empty space within her heart.

As her heartbeat slowed and her senses returned, she let herself fall face first onto the bed. Vykor fell with her, pinning her beneath him for a long moment before he kissed her shoulder and moved to one side, flopping onto the bed, then gathering her into his arms and curling around her.

"Mine." He sounded so smug she had to laugh.

"Was that you or your dragon speaking?"

"Both."

She settled into his arms, eyes closed, body sated. "So, why did you leave today?"

"I got a message from Romak. The temples have learned about me – about us. They basically ordered me to return to Romak. They're sending a ship for us."

A flutter of panic hit. "Romak? They want us to go back?"

"They want a lot of things. I have no intention of giving in to their demands. I gave them enough of my life already. The rest belongs to me."

"And me," she stated, hugging his arms as they held her. "Besides, the Gods sent you to Earth for a reason."

He grumbled. "Maybe. I'm not thrilled about giving the Gods what they want, either."

"What do you want?" she asked.

"You."

She laughed, her heart filling with joy at his simple confession.

"You have me. What else do you want?"

He was silent for a long moment. "It's funny. Until I met you, I would have said the thing I wanted most was to be like other Romaki. I wanted a dragon's spirit, with the magic and clan that came with it."

"And now?" she prompted.

"I have a dragon, but no clan. I have magic, but I'm still unique among my people. I'm a freak, just a different kind, now. But I don't care, because I have you."

He hugged her tighter to his chest. "All I really want is a chance to make a life with you, *razdi*. The priests were the ones that taught me to control my emotions, to hide my disappointment and anger. If they'd been kinder, or less convinced they were right about me, then my dragon might have manifested sooner. I locked him away, Lily. I did that to him, and to us. I don't want anyone to take away any more of my choices. Or yours, for that matter. I want us to be free."

"So, stay on Earth. Our friends want us to stay. We're both needed here. You have no clan, right?"

He nodded. "No clan ever claimed me."

"Then you don't have a ruler to answer to. No one can tell you what to do. They didn't want you before, they can't have you, now." She turned onto her back and smiled up at him. "You're mine."

He kissed her tenderly. "My mate is as wise as she is beautiful." He paused for a moment. "All my life, I've been on my own. It will take some time for me to remember that I'm not alone anymore. I forgot that, today, and I left you. I will not forget again." He touched his chest. "You're part of me, now. Our souls are bound together forever. For this life, and the next."

She put her hand over his. "I've never said this to any other man, and now I know I'll never say it to anyone but you. I love you, Vykor. In this life, and the next."

He stared down at her, eyes gleaming. "You are my guiding star, Lily Ashton, and I love you, too."

EPILOGUE

"THE DELEGATION from Romak is expected to make it to Pyros three days after we arrive," Commander Kash Denza informed the group as they finished the first of what Lily expected to be many meetings. They were seated around a table in a cozy meeting room aboard the *Firebrand*. The king had sent the flagship of his fleet to transport Lily and her friends to Pyros.

"Three days? I thought they'd be waiting to pounce the moment we set foot on the planet," Vykor said.

"They might be under the impression we're arriving a few days later. Space travel is tricky." Kash didn't grin, but the corners of his mouth turned up for a brief second.

"And Prince Radek thought you and Lily might prefer to meet with him, first. Alone," Gwen, Kash's lovely mate, chimed in. She didn't bother hiding her amusement.

"I'd like that." So far, Lily had liked everyone she'd met, both at the embassy and onboard the ship.

"We're going to be busy with Haven business, too," Hanna said. "Lots to be done."

"And when the Romaki delegation does get there, Karos and I will be with you." Megan winked at her. "Just in case they forget that you're not interested in going back to Romak."

"They better not," Vykor rumbled gruffly.

Lily took his hand and squeezed it. "If they do, we'll just remind them that by their own laws, we're not bound by the commands of either clan or the temples." Neither clan had wanted to lay claim to Vykor as a child, which meant that now, he owed fealty to no one.

"They won't try anything on Pyros, either. Arranging to meet on neutral ground was a smart move," Kash said.

"Prince Radek is a smart male," Jet said. "I'm looking forward to meeting him."

Hanna nodded. "As am I."

"I want to meet everyone," Lily said, smiling. "There's so much we still need to learn about the relocation process, what it's like for those of you who have been through it." She nodded to Gwen in acknowledgement. Gwen had been one of the first human women to be claimed by the Pyrosians. With two daughters and a life on Pyros, she knew better than most what to expect.

The meeting broke up shortly thereafter, which

meant she and Vykor finally had a few minutes alone for the first time since coming aboard.

"Come on, Cupcake, time to go to our room." She tapped her leg, and the massive dog lumbered to her feet and padded over to join them.

"You'd think none of them had ever seen a dog before." Lily watched with amusement as several Pyrosian personnel sidled up to the wall as she and Vykor made the walk back to their quarters.

"They haven't. None of them have ever been to Earth." He leaned down to scratch Cupcake's massive head. "And even if they'd visited, none of them are likely to have seen anything quite like our girl."

"True." She'd loved watching Vykor and Cupcake bond over the last few months. He was quite smitten with the dog, and she was equally as taken with him. She'd settled into her new life as the unofficial mascot of the Pyrosian embassy as if she'd been born for the role. Lily smiled a little. Knowing the way the Gods worked? Maybe she had been.

"Have you heard from the Pyrosian historians today?" she asked.

"I did. They're intrigued with my theory and are going through their records, looking for any colony ships that went missing during the time Atlantis was purported to exist."

"Any chance you can meet with them this trip? I'm going to be busy working with Hanna and Megan on the Haven stuff. You'll have time."

"A partner's work is never done," he teased.

"It really isn't." Hanna had made both her and Megan partners. She'd said the Pyros project was too big for just one person, and she'd been right. There was enough work to keep all three of them busy for years to come.

They reached the door to their quarters. Vykor opened it, then stood aside for her to enter. Once she and Cupcake were inside, he joined them, still talking.

"I'd like to set up a meeting with them, then. If they can find correlating data, it would go a long way to proving my theory that the Pyrosians and Romaki were on Earth at the same time, maybe even working together."

"You chase your dreams, I'll chase mine, and we'll meet at the end of the day to exchange stories?" She asked.

"Sounds perfect."

Perfect was a good word to describe her life of late. She had her friends, a new job, Vykor's love and support, and a life she couldn't have imagined a few months ago. The Humanity First movement was gone, and now that she was in full control of her powers, she wasn't afraid of anything anymore. Well, nothing except for the occasional spider that made its way inside the embassy. Those, she still needed Vykor to deal with. There were limits, after all.

"Do you think the delegation from Romak will cause us any real problems?"

"They'll try and push us into going back, but they can't force us. No matter what message they want to send to the populace, holding us against our will won't work. Symbols of peace or of future domination, either way, they need us to agree to it, and that's not going to happen."

"Never," she agreed.

"I will not return just to be used by the priests or anyone else." He pulled her in close and kissed her tenderly. "Besides, there's very little coffee on Romak. I'm not sure you could live without your lattes."

"I'm going to have to find a way," she muttered.

"Why would you do that? I checked. This vessel has a full complement of human foods and beverages."

"Oh, I have my reasons. Before I tell you, I have a question."

"Tease. What's the question?" He grinned down at her, looking happier and more at peace than ever.

In the months they'd been together, they'd made progress both in their own journeys and as a couple. She loved him to the point of madness, which would have been terrifying, save for the fact he felt the same way about her. "How many Romaki does it take to become a clan?"

He blinked at her. "To make a new clan? There have only ever been two, so I don't know if it's ever been considered. I'm sure it would take more than two, though."

She wrapped her arms around his waist and smiled, suddenly feeling shy about her news. "What about three?"

"Three?" His puzzlement slowly changed to shock, then joy. "Three," he repeated again in an awed tone.

"Mmhmm." She bounced on her toes, too excited to stay still any longer. "You're going to be a *tano*."

"A father. I'm going to be a father!" He lifted her into the air and spun her around. "We're going to be a family."

"More than that, love. Soon, there will be another clan of dragons."

He stared up at her, mouth open. "Gods, there will be! The priests are going to lose their minds."

"They can lose whatever they want. We don't answer to them. They're Fire and Snow's problem."

"Yes, they are. Our clan will be based here, on Earth." He set her down and kissed her. "Our clan will need a name, little mother."

"It will. I haven't had much time to think about it, but…what about the Storm Dragon Clan? You know, because of the lightning?" She made a sizzling noise and zigzagged her hands through the air.

"Storm?" He thought about it for a moment, then nodded. "It's a strong name for a strong clan."

She beamed. "the strongest!"

He kissed her again, slow, hot, and hungry. "Tell me, my *razdi*. How long have you known?"

"A few hours."

"But we've been on the ship for half a day, at least, and you have been by my side most of that time…" He frowned. "Except when you went to speak to the medics on board in case the journey made you ill."

"Ista, she's the chief medic here, ran some tests to see why I get motion sick. Turns out, there was a slight irregularity in one of the neural pathways connected to my inner ear. She fixed it for me, and then she looked at the rest of the tests and noticed some elevated hormone readings. I'm about nine weeks along."

"Nine weeks?" He grinned. "Wasn't that around the time you ran out of your prescription and missed a few days?"

"It was. And I told you we'd need to use condoms, and you told me that whatever happened, it was the Gods' will." She laughed. "Seems like they had more planned for us than we knew. You're really okay with this? I mean, we haven't been together long, and parenthood… neither of us had much in the way of role models."

Vykor cupped her face in his hands and met her gaze, his beautiful eyes gleaming with love. "I'm sure. You will be an amazing mother because you will love this child with all of your heart."

"And you will love them just as much. That's a pretty good start for any kid, right?"

"Indeed, it is. And they will have an entire community of humans, aliens, and one very large, grumpy Romaki to help raise them."

"Plus Keth and Eva. The twins Hanna is helping them adopt will arrive before our little one is born. That should give them enough time to start figuring out this parenting thing, right?"

"If not, we can learn together."

She liked that idea. "I can't wait to tell her. We're all going to be parents together!"

"We are." He scooped her into his arms and walked over to the viewscreen on one wall. It showed a view of Earth, which was little more than a bright blue marble in a sea of stars. "That's our home, *sadina*. We will return here to raise our family and live our lives as we choose."

She settled into his arms, basking in the glow of his love as they watched Earth slowly fade from view. It didn't bother her as much as she'd expected, and she knew why. "Earth is where we live, my love. But it's not where my home is. From the moment you claimed me, my home has been with you."

He rumbled deep in his chest, and his next words came out with the roughened tone she knew meant his dragon was present. "And since the moment I saw you standing out in the rain, my heart has been with you."

"*Ours,*" her dragon muttered in contentment.

"*Ours,*" she agreed. Her life was fuller than she'd ever imagined it could be, and the adventure was only just beginning. She had Vykor, her dragon, her friends, now a child to raise in love, laughter, and hope.

"I love you, Vykor Halek of the Storm Dragon Clan."

He stilled for a moment, then nodded. "And I love you, Lily Ashton. From now until the last star fades."

The End

Want to read more stories with book boyfriends
that are out of this world?

**Check out Susan Hayes' other Science Fiction
Romance Titles**

The Drift
Double Down
All In
Wild Card
Three of a Kind
No Limit
Blind Bet
Aces Over Queen

Nova Force
Operation Phoenix
Operation Cobalt
Operation Fury

3013: The Series
3013: RENEGADE
3013: STOWAWAY
3013: TARGETED
3013: FATED
3013: SCARRED

www.ingramcontent.com/pod-product-compliance
Lightning Source LLC
Chambersburg PA
CBHW021151190726
48288CB00008B/2930